my PUCKING Life

ISBN 978-1-964220-12-3 Paperback
ISBN 978-1-964220-13-0 Hardback
ISBN 978-1-964220-11-6 ebook

Edited by Jaquelyn Vale, She Who Edits LLC
Cover Designs by Izzy Elliott (cartoons by @ArtByToniii) and Aurelia Dunbar of Mayonaka Designs
Formatting by Aurelia Dunbar of Mayonaka Designs

Published by Izzy Elliott

To every little girl who believed in soulmates and Prince Charming and grew up to love fated mates and grown-up fairytales.

Note from the Author

Dear Reader,

Before you continue!
My Pucking Life is Book 3 in the Pucking Werewolves series and is the IMMEDIATE continuation of My Pucking Family. This book begins in Leera's immediate next POV.

My Pucking Mate and My Pucking Family should be read first, as this is an ongoing storyline and not interconnected standalones.

We're all standing around Roman in stunned silence. Even the forest seems to hold its breath.

Roman furrows his brows and huffs out a breath of disbelief as he stares at the woman who is claiming to be his sister. "What did you just say?" Roman asks slowly. There's a bite in his words, but it's not anger. It's pain.

She shakes her head, her dark hair mimicking the movement, silently begging to not have to repeat herself.

I can see it now as my eyes continue to volley between Roman and this strange new woman. If you weren't paying attention, it would be easy to miss the small similarities.

"How…how can this be?" he asks, his voice lower and softer than before.

She finally looks up with tear-filled eyes, clearly gauging the situation before her. "I'll tell you everything." Her mouth opens, releasing a small hitched sob. "I'll answer any questions that you may have," she whispers, tears now running down her face with hope reflecting where they had been collecting in her eyes.

I take the single step left between Roman and me, only to place my hand on his arm and let him know I'm here. We all are.

He swings his stricken face to mine and holds his hand over the one I have resting on his arm. He then takes a moment to take in our small group. Our family. Everything we've already overcome to get to this place. The pain and confusion slowly leave his features, replaced with resolve and determination.

He turns and offers her a curt nod. "Yes. You will. But not now." He gestures to the forest around us. "There are more pressing matters."

"Boss…" Dolos trails off. Something seems to be bothering him. Something other than the death and destruction surrounding us, but I don't think Roman notices before he moves towards my soul-brother.

"Khaos, this is your land. What do you want us to do? We're at your disposal."

Khaos is staring across the devastation when we join him on the edge of the clearing. It looks like something out of one of those old war movies my dad liked to watch. A few trees have been uprooted, and there is smoke drifting out of a couple of homes, but the worst part of all of this is the lives lost.

We were so easily distracted by something that, for a moment, we were able to forget that Khaos lost almost his entire pack. There are bodies of all shapes and sizes strewn across the earth, and my heart clenches in my chest as the tears return and slowly cascade down my face.

"I'm so sorry I brought this on you." I cry because this is all my fault. Just like all of the other bad things that have happened in my life…in their lives…It's all because of me. "No," is all Khaos says for a long time. Still staring at the loss of his pack, he continues quietly, "The only beings responsible for this are the ones that ordered the attack and the ones who carried it out...We will find them, and we will stop them."

I can't help but swing myself around Roman and barrel into Khaos' arms. "I know you say that, and deep down, I know you're right, but I still feel responsible. What can we do?"

He doesn't answer. I can't imagine the thoughts flooding his brain. The pain surrounding us is nearly visible to me, and I didn't even know these people. These families. These souls. What he must be feeling as their Alpha must be unbearable. All those broken bonds. All those souls lost.

"Roman, do werewolves have special traditions for death?" I want to be sure we honor those that were lost in the most appropriate way. I know that when I was traveling the world with my parents, there were a few tribes or communities that we stayed with that also had special ceremonies in place for the loss of life.

He nods solemnly and guides me away from Khaos to where our small group is scattered around waiting for orders. Slate is watching the twins watch the woman...We didn't even get her name yet. Andrei is watching Roman and me while Benny is walking towards us.

"Yes, we do. It's called a funeral rite. It's been a long time since we've performed one of this size, but, first, we have to build a bed of trees on the earth and then lay the dead on top of it. After that, we gather around and sing a prayer song to the Moon Goddess. We then finish the ceremony by lighting the trees and bodies on fire. This releases the souls to ascend to the Moon Goddess until they are allowed to return to the realms," he explains softly.

It sounds tragically beautiful, and my heart aches at the thought. "So, we need to gather the trees first, then..." I start with a wobble in my voice. *It's time to be strong, Leera. We have to push through this.* "All right, boys, let's put all these muscles to work. Andrei, can you stay with Khaos and help him with whatever he needs?"

He nods and moves to join Khaos.

"The rest of you are with us. We need to clear an area to lay the trees," I barely finish when the men around me chime, "Yes, Luna."

I stop in my tracks and look around at our broken little family.

I hate the way life has battered us since I arrived in their lives, but I'm thankful that we have each other, and at least for now, we're all safe.

It took all day, but we got everything prepared. The sun will be setting soon, and Khaos' pack has been collected and gently placed together on the large bed of trees. The trees and logs used were the downed trees from the attack, as well as what was left of any homes. We also extended the pyre across the bloodied lands in an attempt to cleanse the earth from the evil that occurred here.

We're currently all standing together on the edge of what will soon be a very large fire. We're quietly waiting for Khaos to be ready to start the prayer song. Roman taught me how to sing the song in their ancient language and translated it for me so that I could participate as well. The tears have already started to collect in my eyes while we wait.

Khaos begins, and we all join in. The feel of their ancient language feels strangely familiar as it rolls off my tongue. The words also morph into howls here and there as we croon through the words.

With these flames,
We beseech you,
Revered Moon Goddess.
Accept those we lost,
Into your secure embrace.
Cleanse their souls of pain,
Preserve their light until the time,
The restoration of their existence,
Reaccompanies us in the realms.

The final word becomes a full howl that I can feel down to my bones. My wolf's sorrow even feels heavy. As the sounds of our howls are carried away by the cool wind, Khaos leans forward to light the fire. We all arrange ourselves around him to support him. I reach for his right hand, the other woman on his left, Roman just behind me with his hand on his right shoulder, and fanned across the rest of the space behind him is the rest of our men have a hand laid across the expanse of his shoulders. The small group of women and the healer we brought with us are just behind the men.

Not one of us stands here with dry eyes.

We stand together, just like this, crying and waiting for the flames to die.

The air around me feels crackly, and as the last flame slows to an ember, I get the strangest, most overwhelming sensation, causing me to gasp and fall to the ground.

All at once, I feel as though dozens of souls have swirled around me, hugging and touching me. I swear a couple of them stopped to look me right in the eye. I can vaguely hear Roman and the men trying to call to me. I don't think they can even touch me through the energy of the souls. My wolf feels like she has her head thrown back, lifted to the sky, with her eyes closed.

Does she know what's happening right now?

She huffs at me, which I interpret as, *Duh.*

Just as quickly as they ascended upon me, they swirl around me a final time and lift into the sky and into the Goddess' arms.

2
ROMAN

The somber moment is broken when Leera falls to the ground all of a sudden. Not only does she fall to the ground, but there is something keeping us from reaching her. Khaos, Andrei, and I are in a panic, yelling her name and trying to reach her, but there's an energy field around her that won't allow us to grasp her.

A strange breeze passes, feeling as though it's moving towards the sky, and I collapse into Leera's space.

"Leera, baby, say something. Are you okay?" I nearly beg.

She sits up and looks around at us like she's hoping we know what the fuck just happened. "I…I think I'm okay…um…I'm going to go out on a limb here and say that doesn't usually happen?"

I shake my head, watching her every move, making sure she's really okay. There's no sign of distress; her anxiety doesn't even seem to be peaked. There's no negative energy coming from her wolf to indicate something bad happened, or my wolf would also be losing his shit.

Leera crawls into my lap, clenching my shirt in her hands. I believe she's just going to sit there holding me when she finally breaks the silence and says, "I think…shit, I must be crazy…I think the souls of the lost were…thanking me?" She lifts her chin, and her confused icy-blue eyes meet mine. "I don't know how else to explain it. It felt like they were wrapping themselves around me, almost hugging me. Why would they thank me? They died because of me. Roman, what's happening to me?" Her voice cracks at the end of her sentence, and the anxious uncertainty I was originally expecting has finally caught up with her. Her forehead crashes against my chest as the tears begin to fall.

"Princess, look at me," I ask gently, lifting her head and wiping her tears away with my thumbs. "Like every other thing we've encountered together, I don't know what's happening right now, but we will find out. I promise. We have a lot of information to unpack together." I pause, looking around our small group, taking in the moment before I say, "But for right now, let's get home." I lift her into my arms and stand. "Khaos, where do you need to be? Do you want to come back with us, or do you need to get back to your team?"

I can't fucking fathom what he's going through right now. His entire pack is gone. I know he's not the most caring asshole out there, but he was their alpha nonetheless. The physical effects of the broken bonds would be excruciating before you even consider how he's feeling.

All the while, it's still active hockey season, and like our team, his is made up of mostly lone wolves who aren't into the "ancient" pack life traditions—their words, not mine. While I understand life in the human realm is vastly different than our heritage, I would never be able to give up the very things that make us who we are. With everything life's been throwing at us this year, it's hard to even think about hockey, if I'm being honest. For so long, it was the escape from my mind that I needed to free myself from reality. Now, I have Leera, and I want to devote every minute to her, but I can't just go awol in the middle of the season, at the height of my career. *Fuck, how I want to, though.*

Khaos answers, watching Leera intently, "I'd like to go where she goes at the moment. I want to be sure she's okay, and I feel as though I've missed something…something feels off."

Which reminds me that we haven't been able to tell him what we learned at her first transition, or even about her transition and meeting her wolf for the first time. I offer him a nod.

"Also to accompany"—he throws his head in the direction of the only surviving member of his pack—"as I assume you have a lot to talk about," Khaos continues, and I acknowledge him with another curt nod.

We all begin to move quietly out of the wooded area, and fuck, there's just so much baggage to unpack when we get home.

Jeanine, thank you for all your help. Would you like one of the men to escort you all home safely?

Alpha, you don't have to thank me for this, not this, but yes, this time I would feel more comfortable if one of your strapping young men could join us.

Slate, please accompany Jeanine and the others to make sure they're safe. Meet with Brutus and ensure the pack is prepared for the possibility of an attack. I want security on high alert. I don't think we need to relocate them; this seemed to be a targeted attack.

Yes, Boss.

Meredith, I know you just got home, but we could really use you back at the townhouse. Slate is going to make sure that Jeanine and the others get home safely. You can either return with him or head that way.

I'll wait for Slate; better safe than sorry.

I caught Leera up on everything that I had just organized through the mind-link, and she nodded, nestling further into my embrace.

One flight, where I dozed off holding Leera while she slept, and a short car ride later, we're finally home.

We all walk through the doors in collective quiet, and Matilda comes scurrying towards us. I think she's going for Benny or me but skips us entirely and makes a beeline for Leera, wrapping her in a motherly hug that only she can provide. "Oh, my sweet dear, are you all right? Meredith got me caught up on everything," she coos and attends to Leera's needs before throwing a look at me over her shoulder, "She said Slate would be there any minute and that they would head this way."

Thank you, Matilda.

Leera sniffles and holds tighter to our little housekeeper. "I'll be okay, Miss Tilly, but you missed quite a bit. There's so much we learned, and there's still so much more we don't even know." She shakes her head like she still can't believe all the shit that keeps happening to her. Honestly, I can't either.

Matilda leads Leera, and therefore all of us, slowly towards the kitchen island, where I notice we suddenly have more barstool chairs than before. She catches me noticing and elaborates, *Slate gave me a few heads up as well,* she finishes, eyes darting briefly towards Khaos and the woman I'm supposed to believe is my sister.

Again, all I can offer is a nod. Words are just too much right now. The competing emotions are so strong that I fear if I open my mouth and begin voicing my concerns and frustrations, I won't be able to stop, and now is not the time for me to unravel. Leera needs me whole.

"Well, then, it sounds like we're in need of some extra sweet coffee and some snacks while you guys tell me all about everything." She hadn't even finished her sentence when she began bustling around the room, gathering snacks.

I decide to help by making Leera one of those decadent iced coffees she loves. I found a new recipe on the Pinterest that everyone says is comparable to those café coffees. While I busy myself with preparing the espresso shot for her coffee, Leera also regains herself and moves into the kitchen. It's then that I realize that the act of enjoying the snacks and drinks themselves was not the only way to bring comfort. For Leera, she enjoys busying herself in the kitchen with Matilda regularly. It gives her mind something to do other than spiral and wander to places it doesn't need to be. She's working beside her now, swaying her hips unconsciously while she works, and you can see the muscles in her face relaxing and giving in to the unique form of therapy.

When the espresso machine finishes sputtering out my little mate's liquid gold, I combine it with the mixture of syrups and sauces I had delivered to recreate all her favorite coffees. With the coffee concoction thoroughly mixed, I pour it over ice in a tall, reusable Cool Beans Coffee tumbler that Leera had brought with her when she moved her stuff in.

While she's still working on making a massive snack spread with Matilda, I slowly step up behind her, grazing her lower back with my left hand as I lean around her right side to hand her the iced coffee. I watch intently as she tastes it, watching for any signs of disinterest; instead, her eyes light up, and she looks at me with her first real smile in far too long.

"Roman, that's so good! Where did you learn how to make this? I've never even been able to figure it out," she huffs in mock irritation, her eyes brightening and sparkling up at me.

"A magician never reveals his secrets," I whisper, kiss her on the temple, and return to my seat at the island with Benny, trying to avert my eyes from the woman who claims to be my sister.

I know I need to talk to her, but where do I even start? What do I even say? Everyone is so somber and quiet; it's weird. Even the twins are looking a little green. Benny looks a little duller than usual, but he'll be okay. Andrei is watching Leera with a worry line stretched across his forehead. Khaos and *my sister*…are sitting on the furthest end of the island, not saying much.

"I—" I'm cut off by Leera's sweet voice.

"Okay, boys—oh, uh, and lady…girl…chick…We'll figure that out later—time to eat. Everyone eat all you need; we'll make more if we need to." She smiles warmly at us all with a worry line, matching Andrei's, also stretched across her forehead. It's the Luna in her, wanting to take care of her people. Her family. Our family.

I extend my hand to her, and when she takes it, I pull her around the island and onto my lap.

"Roman, I can sit on my own," she gasps.

"I know you can, but I like you right where you are. Now start eating." I've already started piling food onto her plate. Small sandwiches, a scoop of the mixed fruit they had cut, a small salad, some crackers, and summer sausage. When her plate is towered with more food than she'll probably be able to eat, I begin filling mine.

While everyone eats, the life and light slowly return to each person in the room. Benny's smile slowly grows. The twins look a little less green. Even Khaos looks a lot like he's found his hope that everything could be okay moving forward. Leera's infectious, peaceful presence settles around me. Andrei sighs, releasing some of the tension and worry tethered around his body. I try not to notice even the woman's face at the end of the table looks a little brighter.

Matilda's eyes catch mine as I survey the only people in all the realms that I care about, nodding with a sweet smile that says everything will be okay, and I allow myself a moment to believe it.

3
Leera

Not only did we make it through all of the first round of snacks that Miss Tilly and I made, but we refilled it twice before everyone had had their fill. While it all definitely helped brighten everyone's moods a minuscule amount, it was still a little somber and borderline uncomfortably quiet, but I know everyone is just trying to unpack everything we've encountered.

Now, we're all sitting around, stomachs full and safe, but no one is breaking the growing silence.

"Okay, so…How about we all get some much-needed showers and rest? Then, we can all meet up in the morning to discuss everything"—I twist my head, my eyes meeting Roman's before moving to our new guest from Khoas' pack—"and make a plan to move forward."

Benny slaps his hands against the top of the island as he springs from his seat. "Sounds like a plan. Night, everyone!" And just like that, he's bounding down the hall towards his door as the rest of the room slowly rises.

As much as I want to drag Roman away, I also have this need

to be sure everyone is settled in and has what they need. Slate and Andrei are the next to call it a night. After everyone has made their way to their rooms, I begin to hear water running throughout the townhouse as everyone prepares to cleanse themselves of everything we encountered. Khaos finishes saying a few words to the woman and then gives me a giant bear hug—or maybe a wolf hug—and quietly walks away. The twins are whispering at each other, and it doesn't look like they're having a pleasant conversation. I don't think I've ever seen them so quiet or irritated with each other—or anyone for that matter.

Roman must also notice it because he cuts off my train of thought when he barks at the twins, "Is something wrong with you two?"

"Yes," "No," they answer in unison, Dolos looking more irritated while Eris looks like someone kicked his pet.

Roman raises a single eyebrow and just stares at them, waiting for one of them to say something, but when no one does, his irritation seems to rise. "I'll give you the night to get your shit together, like everyone else, but you will tell me what's going on with you two in the morning." He leaves no room for discussion and begins to walk away. I can't help but peek around Roman on our way to our room to check on them, finding Dolos watching the quiet woman.

"Are you not going to talk to her at all before tomorrow? Does she even know where she's sleeping?" I know I shouldn't push him, but speaking from experience, finding out you have family that you didn't know existed, especially when you thought you were all alone in the world, you should treasure every moment, no matter how hard it is to face the truths that come with them.

He doesn't immediately answer me, but he does lift me off my feet and crash my body against his chest like he needs to hold on to me, or I could float away.

"Roma-hmph—" I'm cut off with his finger on my lips.

He turns us through the doorway of our room and kicks the door shut behind him before gently setting me on my feet and turning to his dresser, fidgeting with the few things he has sitting on top of it.

"It would seem that you are far stronger than even I gave you credit for…how do you continue to handle this over and over?" He turns toward me with so much pain in his eyes that it makes my knees buckle.

"Oh, Roman." I open my arms to him because I don't trust my legs to carry me across the room. He rushes into me and just holds my body plastered against him with his nose resting in the crook of my neck, just breathing me in.

"I'm here," I soothe, and it's my turn to run my hands up and down his back—like he's done for me so many times. "I'm here, and I'm not going anywhere. And I'd be willing to bet that once you give her a chance, she won't either. I know it's hard. I know it's scary to have someone else to care about. I know it's hard to realize you don't know everything about your own life. But we'll get through this. All of us. Together." I repeat the words he's also told me so many times now.

We stand there just existing and holding on to each other for dear life until I gently pull myself from his embrace and lead him to his bathroom.

When we enter the bathroom, he goes to take charge and prepare everything, but I stop him, "Let me take care of you this time?"

He looks perplexed, like the thought of someone, anyone, taking care of him is such a foreign concept.

"You do know you're allowed to let others care for you as much as you care for them, right?" I whisper softly as I approach him and wrap my arms back around him. I just can't fight the need to be in constant physical contact with him right now, especially when he needs me like this.

I pull back slightly, allowing me to look him in the eye. "We really need to work on sharing those kinds of responsibilities here, okay?"

He nods. "But you've been through far more than me, let me—"

"No. I mean, yes…My shit tends to hit the fan more often and harder, but this is heavier for you, and I want to take care of my…mate." I smile warmly, remembering that using those words can help when I need to get my way, and this is one of those situations.

"That's unsportsmanlike conduct," he says with a sweet smile, peeling his body from mine to allow me to prepare a bubble bath for him. Not only does he need to relax, but I need to see my big, hunky werewolf sitting in a bubble bath.

"Well, if you had just agreed, I wouldn't have had to pull out my secret weapon," I try to say without laughing and fail. I turn the water on nice and hot, adding the same chamomile bubbles he gave me after he rescued me. *How does that already feel like a lifetime ago?*

I dim the harsh white lights in the room to a dreamier aesthetic, lighting a few vanilla candles on the white marble countertops. I get him settled in the bath and lean in behind him to massage his massive shoulders. He slowly melts under my touch and groans when I work out a few especially hard knots, which is actually most of his neck. He's wound so tight I wonder how he's able to move as gracefully as he is, both on and off the ice. He finally sinks into the water on a low groan and gives in to the magic a bubble bath can provide.

I move to step away from him when he gently catches my wrist. "Don't go," his husky voice breaks the silence, begging me with a deep pain and need in his eyes.

Allowing him to pull me back to the tub, I rest my hand on the side of his face and kiss his forehead. "I'll be right back. Please rest."

His eyes search mine before he nods and relaxes his head on the back of the tub, resting his eyes.

I scurry back into the room as quietly as I can, searching for my phone. When I've finally found it, I tip-toe to the bathroom door and line up a perfect picture of Roman in a bubble bath that I will treasure forever. Except I wasn't properly prepared for my covert mission, and when I snap the picture, it makes that god-awful shutter sound that phones make. My cover is blown, and his eyes fly open and catch me ogling him.

Instead of fessing up and brushing it off, I panic and bolt away from the door, like he doesn't know it was me standing there, taking a picture of him. If I could see my wolf right now, I think it's safe to say she'd be rolling her eyes—which she apparently heard me think because she huffs in agreement, causing me to giggle.

"What are you planning on doing with that picture? Is this where you tell me you're really a witch and now you're going to try to blackmail me?" he hollers from the bathroom, and I'm finally able to relax a little at the humor in his voice.

Quick, Leera, how can we distract him from the fact that I just wanted to keep this moment for myself?

The thought is instant, and I grin to myself like an idiot because I'm that proud of myself, but it's a good plan.

After taking a few moments to prepare for my plan of distraction, I ready myself with a deep breath, hoping I can draw some courage from my wolf.

I finally walk through the door of the still dimly lit bathroom. I expected Roman to still be resting with his head against the back of the tub. Instead, he's staring directly at me as I try my best to sway my hips in a sensual way without looking like a waddling duck. I must be doing it right because his eyes look like they're only a second from falling out of his face, and I think he's drooling.

"I was hoping I could join you," I whisper because I used all my courage to walk across the bathroom…naked.

He doesn't answer with his words. He growls and leans over the edge of the tub, reaching for me. Once he's grasped my fingers, he pulls me up against the warm basin before hooking one arm under my legs at the knee and the other on my back, keeping me from toppling over. *I will never get used to how strong he is,* I think as he lifts me into the tub like I weigh nothing at all.

Once he's gently settled me in his lap, resting my back against his torso, he begins massaging my body.

"I'm supposed to be the one taking care of you, remember?" I breathe.

He continues massaging my body, which not only feels amazing but is also setting off every nerve ending in my body at the intimacy of everything.

"But what if me taking care of you calms me and therefore,

in turn, takes care of me?" he grumbles against the shell of my ear, causing my toes to curl and my core to throb.

I open my mouth to speak, but now he's scrubbing my scalp with what feels like his claws, and I have to snap it shut to keep myself from moaning.

"Now who's playing dirty?" I barely get out before I'm unable to hold the moan in any longer, as I arch into him, earning me a growl from him. That's all it takes for our calm bath to turn into frenzied touching.

We hurriedly bathe each other, lathering, scrubbing, and massaging each other's bodies. When we're all clean and have washed the day and recent experiences off our skin, I suggest we move this party to our bed.

He gets out of the tub first and shakes off, which results in a small fit of unexpected giggles as I remember that he's a werewolf. *And I'm a werewolf. Do things like shaking come naturally or are they learned?* I can't help but giggle again at the thoughts that cross my mind.

My thoughts are broken by him lifting me out of the bathwater, desperately clinging to his biceps as they flex beneath my fingers, and there's no way I'm not another kind of wet right now.

He inhales deeply, and I remember that he can smell my arousal, which reminds me that his scent would be stronger as well, I allow myself to concentrate on my wolf and inhale deeply, and I'm immediately overwhelmed with the muskier cherries and leather that I smelled when I went into heat. I was so wrapped up in the moment the other times we were together, I didn't even allow myself to notice the little things. I want to mentally catalog every single moment. Forever.

Being a part of that end-of-life ceremony reminded me that

even if we could live an obnoxious number of years, we're not truly immortal. We can be killed, and…I just…there's no way I could live without him now that I have him.

I have this raging need to be near his neck. I rest my hands on his shoulders, pulling on them a little. "Hold me. Please, Roman."

I didn't need to beg; he was already lifting me into his embrace. As soon as our bodies meet, still slick with bath water, I wriggle and wrap my legs around his waist. He throws his head back on a low, rumbling groan, and I pull myself up to lay my head on top of his shoulder, breathing him in the same way he does me so often.

There's a burning sensation in my gums, and it causes me to whine.

He immediately snaps out of the lust-induced fog and holds my body at arm's length, causing me to whimper. "Oh, sweetheart, I'm sorry. Not yet."

I stop and look at him in confusion, urging him to explain himself.

"That need you were feeling was to complete the mating bond; if you had bitten me, we would have needed to complete the ritual to prevent an unintentional rejection," he explains calmly while he begins to play my body like his own personal instrument again, which delays the gravity of what he just said.

"Wait, what? I would never reject you." I'm volleying between panic over his statement, and need because of the things he's doing to my body.

He rolls my nipple between his thumb and forefinger and my knees shake without my permission.

"I know you wouldn't Princess, but an incomplete mating bond can cause it to reflect as a rejection. I just want it to be perfect for you, and that's my fault for not explaining that before." He leans in and begins kissing across the same spot on my shoulder, and I can feel my need for him beginning to collect on my thighs. "But I'm still going to take care of you."

He says that, but the second the word left his mouth, all of his heat left my body, and he walked into the bedroom without me, leaving me standing there gaping at him, I'm sure.

"I didn't want to carry you again and make it worse. Come here, Leera." His voice has taken on a firmer tone, and the collection of moisture is now sliding down my legs as I make my way to him.

He's sitting against the headboard again, just watching me try to saunter towards him. He reaches between his legs and maintains a steady grip on his length, occasionally stroking it slowly, his eyes never leaving mine.

When I approach the bed, instead of walking around to the side and joining him, I begin at the end of the bed and crawl to him. Just as I reach him, I intend to reach out and touch him, but he anticipates my move and captures my hand. In a quick series of obnoxiously graceful maneuvers, he has me turned around, on my knees, facing away from him. He leans over me, and I can feel him brush against my sensitive skin, causing me to whimper again, "What do you want?" he asks while he reaches around my body, teasing my nipples.

My back arches, and my head falls back against him. "You, Roman," I breathe. "I don't want you," I continue to pant, but his hand stills at my words when I remember I wasn't finished with my sentence. "It's not a want…I…I need you."

He releases a ragged sigh of relief, immediately followed by a trail of kisses down my spine, causing me to wriggle in his grasp.

"Mine," he growls, and I again feel the heat of his body leave mine, but only for a moment. He plunges his face into my dripping and sensitive skin, and I cry out in pleasure. The new angle offering a completely new range of stimulation as he licks my entire slit and then pays extra attention to my clit. My arms and legs are shaking, and I can no longer hold the weight of my head, letting it hang between my shoulders as I pant and moan and cry his name.

Just when it feels like the world will fall away and the pleasure will consume me, he pulls away, leaving me a whimpering mess of skin and bones, my soul having already left my body in preparation of the impending orgasm.

"Roman, please!" I beg shamelessly.

He reaches around me, using each breast as an anchor for his grip, and pulls me up so that my back is plastered against his front, and the throb between my legs being brushed with the head of his cock is the sweetest kind of torture.

"Do you trust me?" he breathes against the shell of my ear.

I'm nodding frantically both because I do trust him blindly—with my mind, body, heart, and soul—but also because I really want to feel those fireworks dancing across my skin.

"Tell me, Princess," I would almost think he's unbothered by all of this intimacy if it wasn't for the way his dick twitches against me while he lazily trails his fingers all over my body, except exactly where I want it.

"Yes, mate, I trust you with all I am. Now, please let me come," I whine impatiently.

He reaches forward and bands one arm around my middle, almost completely holding me up, and then I feel him reach between us and grab his length. For a tiny, minuscule moment,

I feel a small spark of fear at not being prepared for this. I know I want to complete the mate bond, but he said we weren't doing that tonight.

Now I'm just confused, which he must feel through the bond because he continues to lazily stroke himself when he explains, "Just because we're not taking that final step tonight doesn't mean you can't come all over my cock, my little miracle."

Now I'm even more confused, but a shiver of anticipation skitters through my body when he finally lowers his hard dick between my legs, but he doesn't enter me. He starts moving in short, slow movements through the wetness still gathering in my core. The friction and the lightning shooting through my body at the contact are enough to cause me to pant and moan again. But he's not done with me yet. His short and slow movements across my center become long and languid strokes that are now creating the same delicious friction against that beautiful bundle of nerves, and I grip onto him for dear life.

"Oh my God, Roman…" I had another thought after that, but my body took over, and I couldn't stop the moan that escaped me. Every orgasm with this man felt like I was being destroyed and remade all at once, and this one would be the most intense yet. "…P-please, don't stop this time." To reinforce my need for this release, I begin to rock my hips with him, finding my own ways to draw out the most amazing sounds from him.

He slows and allows me a moment to take over while I continue grinding against him, bringing us both unparalleled pleasure. He removes the arm he has banded around me and moves both of his hands to grip my hips, and the feel of him holding me like this urges me on.

"Yes…Fuck, Leera…You're fucking perfect. Come for me,

Princess," he pants in my ear, trailing kisses along my neck, nipping as he goes.

"Oh gods…Roman. I'm almost there…I can't…" My movements become frenzied and completely out of control, but the wave is cresting over me, and I want to ride it all the way to the top.

Roman is practically roaring behind me, his grip on my hips tightening, sending even more electricity to my body. Without warning, my entire being implodes, and the shockwaves consume me. I'm fairly certain I'm screaming, but I can't be bothered to care right now. My vision turns white, and Roman catches me when my body slumps against him. He jerks a few more times and groans into my neck, saying my name like a prayer.

I must have passed out because I don't remember being laid on a pillow, but I'm awakened by a warm, rough feeling between my legs. My head feels heavy, but I lift it enough to see him cleaning me up. I don't even have the energy to thank him because I fall back to the pillow, sleep trying to claim me once more. The next thing I know, I feel his large, warm body pulling me into his embrace and wrapping around me.

Before I give all the way in to the darkness, my last thought is that every horrible thing I've ever had to go through, and likely still have to go through, will be worth it if it's my payment for having him as my mate and life partner.

4
ROMAN

Watching Leera sleep has become one of my favorite pastimes. It's not as high up on the list as making her scream my name or anything, but it still brings me peace and happiness. Knowing she's really here. That this is all really happening. As if it wasn't enough that the Goddess returned my mate to me, and she has all these abilities that we don't understand, but now I have a sister that I didn't know about. Not even a half-sister. That would make more sense because I never exactly pegged my father as the loyal type. No, this woman has my mother's features.

Thinking back, I don't even entirely know how my mother died. I was still quite young for a werewolf. Father told me that she was ill and it overtook her, but I learned from those close to her that the illness he's referring to was depression and not the chemical imbalance kind that so many beings suffer from. It was due to the constant abuse from my father. Not physical abuse, because that's beneath even him. Mental warfare is his preferred game of choice. He tried it on me and was successful at times, more than I'd like to admit.

I knew she wasn't happy with him, but he was her fated mate. He was supposed to make her happy and keep her safe, and he didn't do either. I was so young; I don't know much more about their relationship outside of the snarky remarks he would throw at her, some so sharp that she would visibly flinch like he had hit her. I hated him. I wanted to rip his head from his body the few times he did it in front of me, but she'd get upset and stop me. Beg me not to allow him to turn me into a monster.

Thinking back to the way my father manipulated my life and the fact that I grew into almost exactly who he wanted me to be almost makes me feel guilty. The only thing that saves me is knowing I did it all my way, without his darkness fueling me. I kept my mother's kind words tucked inside my heart and never let them go. Sure, I've had to do some atrocious things as the captain of a werewolf army, but those things were done for the greater good and protection of our people. Not for the evil and dark-hearted.

Would my mother be proud of the man I've become? She would have adored Leera. How could she keep my sister from me? Why didn't my sister seek me out? Does she believe me to be like my father? Is she in danger?

The worry and nagging thoughts continue to spiral through my mind. I pull Leera even farther into my embrace. I wish I could carve a Leera-sized hole in my body and keep her with me always. Keep her safe. But that's not how the world works, and she's in danger.

I try to quiet the turbulence that has become my brain for another hour before I give up and slip out of bed, careful not to wake my sweet little mate. She whimpers in her sleep, causing me to flinch, stop, and tuck her in tightly before turning towards the door.

Swiping a pair of gray sweatpants from my drawer, I step into them quickly and reach for the doorknob. Turning to check on her one more time before I allow myself to leave the room, I close the door quietly behind me. She has a tendency to untuck herself in her sleep, and I don't need one of the men to see her naked. Her poor brothers would be scarred.

I walk the quiet halls of the townhouse and stop in the kitchen for a couple of bottles of water before making my way to the gym. I would usually just let my wolf loose to run it off, but that's not an option right now. I don't want to leave Leera when she's in danger and still unable to communicate telepathically with me.

The thought of claiming her, of finally completing the mate bond, threatens to send too much blood where it's not currently needed. I shake away the thoughts of her body and take the final steps to the gym when I notice the light is shining through the space between the floor and the door.

I must not be the only one who couldn't sleep.

Opening the door and stepping inside, I surprise myself by laughing when I see all the men currently under my roof in the gym. Most are working out, but Eris still looks to be moping about something.

Benny stands and drapes his arm around my shoulders with his signature shit-eating grin on his face. "Now that the boss is here, we can have a party!" he hollers and whoops around like an idiot.

I roll my eyes to make a show of my expected annoyance, but I'd be lost if my best friend ever lost his light. "Is it really a party if everyone's here because they can't sleep? Which…why is everyone else, other than Khaos and Andrei, here?" I look around the room suspiciously. *What is bothering all of my men so badly that they can't sleep?* "All right, out with it. Don't make me pull rank. What's going on?" My voice ends softer than I usually use with my men, but I've learned that even as werewolf men, Leera has taught me that it's okay to be more than what's expected of us.

So, while I am still their Alpha that can and will kill to protect those that I love, they are also my best friends. When no one answers, I walk over to the pull-up bar and drop both bottles of water onto the floor next to me and continue, "I'll start then…" *Why do men make talking about what we're going through so difficult?* I reach up, wrapping my hands around the pull-up bar, and begin lifting my body, talking between reps, "I'm concerned about all these powers Leera has that we don't understand…I'm constantly on alert because she's in danger…I want to murder my father for killing Khaos' pack…I'm afraid to get to know my sister and have someone else to care about…I don't know if I'm ready to learn what I didn't know about my mother and father…I'm weirded out about why Eris and Dolos—I fix them with a stern glance—are acting strange…fuck." I finish, dropping to the floor and retrieving one of the bottles of water to chug until it's empty and crinkling it in my grasp.

For an uncomfortably long time, no one says anything, and I think that I got too touchy-feely with them. I'm surprised that it's Khaos that speaks up first, "I don't know what to do…" Everyone stops what they're doing, waiting for him to continue. When I spoke, they kept about their workouts as I was, but now we're all giving him our undivided attention. "At the end of the day, I always had my pack, my people…Hockey is fun and all, but it was just an outlet; it didn't bring me the peace and the closest thing to happiness I'd felt in, well, most of my life…I can't believe

Runa is your sister…I—"

"Runa?" I interrupt with fire burning the back of my throat.

His eyes widen when he realizes that was the first time I'd heard her name, and then he nods.

"Runa means…" I trail off, unable to finish my sentence.

"Yes, Runa means secret in the ancient language, but that's all I know. I would assume it's intentional, but I don't know more about the situation. That's for us to learn in a couple hours, it would seem."

I walk over and grab a towel off of one of the shelves to wipe the sweat from my face. "I interrupted you. Continue." I nod towards Khaos as I begin gathering weights for the bench press.

"I can't believe the King's advisor had his own daughter killed…I'm worried about Leera—we just got her back…and I'm ready to be caught up on all the shit you said I missed and what's going on with her." Now that he's finished talking, he walks up to the treadmill to run while we all continue discussing everything that's going on.

Andrei rises to his feet. "I guess this is as good a time as any for me to take over. I just wanted to say, 'I'm sorry' again, Roman, I couldn't tell you until I was sure." He swings his head to me, and I nod, letting him know I'm not upset with him. He then swings his head to Khaos, who is no longer running. He's straddling the treadmill belt, waiting for what Andrei has to say next. "I suspected it from the first time I met her, but Leera is not only my twin sister…she's also the lost princess of Zabella. You would have felt the royal shift."

"WHAT?!" Khaos roars at us all, "How in the actual fuck does this shit keep getting worse?! I thought I felt it, but I hadn't stopped to think what it meant. She doesn't have to be a fucking princess if she doesn't want to be!" he growls and begins to pace.

"She won't," Andrei and I answer in unison, and I continue, "We've already told her that. It's her choice, but with the current state of things, she's considering embracing it if it means taking down whatever plans mine and India's father have laid out. From what we've been told so far, it's not good, and we have a lot of information that we still need to collect."

Khaos looks a little calmer, but he's definitely still wound tight and ready to fight at the drop of a hat.

"So, I guess I'm mostly worried about Leera and her new powers and reuniting her with our parents," Andrei finishes with the things currently weighing heavy on his shoulders when Khaos asks, "Hold on. The King and Queen didn't have just one child? They had twins? Why didn't you take your place as the heir to the throne then?"

Andrei takes a few moments to catch Khaos up on the full description of the situation that he explained to all of us at the full moon ceremony while we all continue working through our frustrations on the gym equipment.

When they've finished, Benny looks towards the twins and Slate, as if gauging to see if one of them wishes to speak, and shrugs when they don't. "My turn, I guess." He smiles. "I'm worried about Leera's safety and happiness through all this crap she keeps going through…I'm irritated that all of this is making it hard to want to focus on hockey…I'm really just tired of everything being heavy again…That's why we left…" When he finishes speaking, he shakes it off, moving as though a shiver just shot up his spine, almost as if he's dislodging the negative emotions, and replaces his signature smirk on his face before turning to the twins, "Out with it, you two," he teases.

Dolos opens his mouth to speak, but Eris cuts him off with a look that says he does not want to talk about something.

Benny, have you been able to get either of them to talk to you?

No, Boss, they've both had everyone blocked out since we were at Khaos' pack.

Crossing my arms and watching them clearly mentally argue with each other, I begin to lose my patience. *What the fuck could they have going on that they won't talk to us about it?*

Dolos just shakes his head at his brother before he turns to me. "We've just got some of our own shit we need to sift through. We'll catch you up when we've reached an understanding ourselves."

Eris snatches his hat off the floor, sliding it on backward, and stomps out of the room without a word to anyone, and we all stare at Dolos.

"He'll come around, and then we'll talk about it just…just not yet." He shrugs and ducks his head as he heads after his twin.

All eyes swing to Slate, the last one in the room who hasn't had something to share in our weird men-have-feelings-too discussion. My wolf snorts at me, and I roll my eyes again. Slate finished lifting not long after I entered the gym and has been straddling the bench, tapping away on his laptop ever since. "You'll all be disappointed that I don't have any touchy-feeling things for you. I guess I am a little stressed at not being able to keep a better track on Avram and Boian, but I know our pack. I know us. We'll figure it out. We always do." He never looks at us, still typing wildly on his laptop with his neck craned over the damn thing. Strangely enough, his words, though few, made me feel a little better.

Just to irritate him, I walk over and ruffle all the thick black hair on his head. It works; he lifts his head to shoot me a glare, but when he does, all I say is, "Thanks," and it catches him off guard, and he shrugs it off and returns his attention to this screen.

"Well, boys, I'm feeling a little better…I think. I'm going to return to my mate and try to get a couple hours of sleep before Leera's pow-wow."

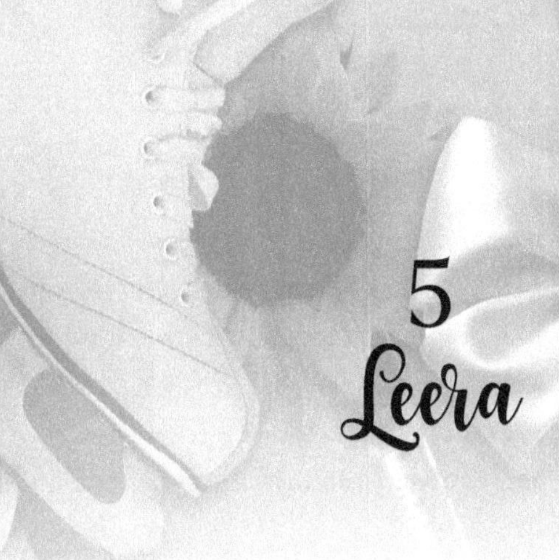

5
Leera

My alarm blares to life, but I'm not able to get up to shut it off. I'm trapped. There is a large muscular arm wrapped around my body, holding me in place. I try to wriggle out from under his arm, which only causes him to tighten his hold on me. While I'd love to stay in his embrace all day, we have an agenda to tackle today, the most important item being learning the hard stuff about Roman's sister, father, and mother.

We haven't really talked about his mother. I know that she died when he was young and that his dad is a royal tool—pun not intended, but appropriate—and not the actual royals' tool, the King's advisor. He spoke of his father's darkness early in our relationship, but I didn't know that meant, like, kidnapper-and-murderer type of darkness. I just thought he meant his dad was an ass, but I should have known that as a werewolf, it would mean so much more.

I'm worried about him. My big man looks tough and strong, and obviously is, but he also uses his hard exterior to hide how much he cares because the things he loves have been taken from him.

Please let his sister be good. I beg any entities listening, and my wolf huffs her approval.

Resuming my wiggling, I manage to turn all the way around to face him. If you didn't know any better, you'd think he was still sleeping, but knowing him, he's been up for ages and is just letting me stare at his stupid handsome face. I gently tap on his forehead, "I'm pretty sure you're awake in there. It's time to get up and face this head-on," I coo as I run my fingers through his nearly shaggy, sandy hair.

He grumbles and cracks one eye open. "I'll never be able to get up and do anything if you keep touching me like that."

"Like what? I was just messing with your hair." I pull back in confusion.

"Haven't you learned that any touch from you ignites a fire under my skin that usually only your sweet little pussy can extinguish," he rasps.

There's no way I'm not fire engine red right now. I swat at his chest in admonishment. "Roman! You can't say things like that!"

He lifts an eyebrow to match his crooked grin. "And why not? It's the truth, and I haven't heard any complaints from you…"

"Well, of course you haven't because…ugh, you know…I just don't want to TALK about it." I giggle and hide under the blankets.

He begins to search for me, and I know I'm in for it when there's a knock at the door. "Five minutes, and I'm coming in to get you, Boss!" Benny's booming voice carries into our room, causing Roman to growl.

I manage to scurry the rest of the way under the covers to the edge of the bed, escaping in a mess of silver hair and missing a fuzzy pink sock. When my feet hit the floor, I spring back up and clap my hands. "All right, let's do this. We might learn some not-fun things today, but we're together, and everything will be okay. Let's tackle this quickly so that we can move on. Plus, you have practice later, so you'll be able to work off any anger that results from what we learn," I finish my mini pep talk with my hands on my hips and my chin held high.

Roman releases a breathy chuckle and slowly rises from the bed. I can see every muscle in his back ripple like water in a lake, and I can't tear my eyes away. "I thought we were getting dressed, Princess."

I scoff and move to the dresser to grab my clothes, doing my absolute best to pretend like he doesn't exist. I slowly peel his shirt from my body and make a show of sliding a bra on before climbing into my favorite black leggings. I finish the look with a Predators hoodie and head into the bathroom for my small morning ritual; it's not long before Roman joins me. We're both brushing our teeth as I swing my hips, thinking I'd just, like, hip bump him, but because of our height difference, I just hit it rock-hard thighs.

How can a man even look handsome smiling with a mouth full of toothpaste? This is ridiculous.

I think back to how apprehensive I was to move in with him, and here we are, brushing our teeth together, getting dressed, dealing with murderers…Okay, the last one sucks, but this whole normal life part is kind of nice. Scratch that, it's really nice. I was so worried about having the normal college girl experience that I forgot to just live the life sitting right in front of me.

"I love you," I blurt with my mouth still full of toothpaste.

"I love you too, Leera. Always. Let's go do this then. Also, there's something waiting for you downstairs."

Okay, because that's not suspicious or anything. Nonetheless, I race him out of the room and downstairs to see what's waiting for me.

6
ROMAN

I know when Leera reaches the kitchen because a happy little squeal echoes throughout the entire house, making me chuckle to myself. I turn the final corner into the main area of our home and sigh with resignation at the information I'm going to learn. The sigh turns into more of a "whoof" sound—not the wolf kind, but the kind when someone surprises you and nearly knocks the wind out of you—because my sweet little mate has barreled into me for a hug.

"Thank you for the coffee and flowers; you really didn't have to do that," she finishes by pulling on my shirt until I've leaned over enough that she thanks me with a kiss that makes me want to throw her over my shoulder and say to hell with all this. When she finally pulls herself from our kiss, her eyes are dazed, and she mutters a breathy, "Thank you, Roman," before returning to her coffee.

I had asked Benny to run and get everyone some coffee but to make sure to get Leera's favorite and some flowers because her last batch had died while we were gone. "Don't I get a hug for getting everything?" Benny teases.

I growl.

Leera giggles.

Slate shakes his head from his perch at the island while keeping his focus on his laptop.

Andrei's clearly still trying to wake up as his coffee cup clings to his mouth, sipping on it as if it's his only hope to stay awake. Khaos saunters into the room, hugging Leera on his way in like he needs to channel some of her sunshine to get through the day.

My sister—Runa—follows closely behind him. I make a conscious effort to not look like an ass when she glances at me, relaxing my forehead where Leera likes to smooth.

The twins are the last ones in the room, and come hell or high water, I will find out what the fuck is up with them after all of this…by any means necessary.

"I br—" Benny begins, but I cut him off.

"I had Benny get coffee if you want some; there are sweet and darker options. You can have as much as you like." I gesture towards the obnoxious amount of Cool Beans Coffee cups all over the kitchen counter with Leera's sunflower bouquet.

Runa nods and says a quiet 'thank you' as she gravitates towards the sweeter coffee options. I catalog that tidbit of information for later as I move towards the giant couch in the living room area. We could all easily fit at the dining room table, but I don't want this to feel like a board meeting or interrogation. I'll save that for the twins. For what we have to discuss, I want us all to be as comfortable as possible.

I sink into the seat on the furthest left side of the couch by the floor-to-ceiling windows. I'm sipping on my coffee when Leera makes it to the couch and moves to sit beside me. I quickly set my coffee down on the sofa table and capture her by the hip, pulling her onto my lap. She squeals but settles in to make herself comfortable. "I need to hold on to you to get through this," I whisper into her hair with my head in the crook of her neck.

She wraps her arm around my head and kisses the side of it, letting me hold onto her as everyone else joins us in the living room.

When my sister makes eye contact with me, I nod and try to smile, "Whenever you're ready," I encourage her.

I'm not ready, but I have to be. I have to know how she exists and why she hid from me for so long.

"Okay, so…I suppose it's best to start at the beginning," Runa begins, wringing her hands in her lap.

"Take all the time you need." Leera smiles at her warmly and encouragingly while the rest of us nod in agreement.

Runa nods, more to herself than anything, and takes a deep breath, gathering herself for what she's about to tell me. For what she's about to tell all of us. "Before I begin, I think it would take a lot of the weight off of my shoulders if I know how you feel about your father."

"Isn't he our father?" I challenge and arch my right eyebrow, testing her reaction to him, and allow myself to smile when she snaps back.

"No, he isn't. His DNA gave me life, but that vile creature is no father of mine. I won't tell you anything else until you tell me how you feel about him." She crosses her arms over her chest and raises her right eyebrow in response, and dammit if that move doesn't create a small fissure in my heart, as if to make room for her.

My smile morphs into a low laugh. "Then we already have

something to agree on. Please continue."

She sighs as if in relief and looks stronger when she begins again, "Well, that man is a monster. You are not their firstborn child. And we are not the only children they conceived."

She must notice I'm about to interrupt her, so she raises her hand, "I know, and I will tell you everything. It's just…It's heavy, and I haven't ever said any of this out loud."

Leera starts rubbing soothing circles on the back of my neck and whispers, "I know this is a lot for both of you, but try to let her get through it, Big Guy," she finishes her thought with a kiss to my temple.

"Also, please remember that all of this was told to me, so there are some details that I may not have or might get slightly wrong…So anyways. Apparently, when they were young, Avram and Boian went to Sabbax and found a dark witch to grant them their prophecies." A gasp sounds from Matilda at the kitchen island. She's resting on her elbows while sipping on one of the sweet coffees.

Leera looks around in confusion, and when no one explains, she asks, "Why did Miss Tilly gasp? I mean, it definitely doesn't sound good, but we've talked about the dark witches before without anyone gasping."

Andrei speaks up to fill her in, "Witches created a law a couple centuries ago that forbids them from casting spells to provide prophecies."

"Why?"

"Because they make people crazy," Benny pipes in and continues, "They obsess over the words, constantly trying to figure them out. If the vision of the future is clear, they lose their minds trying to make sure it does or doesn't come true."

Leera nods, taking in all the new information. "So…India was telling the truth?" she asks the room.

"It would seem so, sweetheart," I soothe because I feel her sadness begin to rise. "Do you know the prophecy?" I ask my sister, but she's already shaking her head.

"I'm sorry, no, just that whatever it is made him decide that he refused to have daughters…" she trails off again and looks to be gathering herself. "In the beginning, when Mother became with child their first time, he used the excuse that he would not have a daughter for an eldest child. She obviously became overwhelmed with fear and sadness because her instincts told her the pup was, in fact, a girl." She stops speaking, eyes on her lap, and chances a look around the room and glances at my men, and I can barely contain my rage.

Leera shoves off my lap and sits between us. "They're not mad at you; just keep going."

"When Mother gave birth, he refused to be with her, so she only had the healer with her. But this wasn't one of the King and Queen's healers that would normally tend to her. This was one paid by Avram to do exactly as he instructed." She takes a deep breath, and I brace myself. "His instruction was that only a male heir was to survive the birth," she whispers sadly, voice shaking.

A collective group of curse words is fired around the room, and the anger from everyone is palpable. I'm shaking with rage, but I need to hear it all. "Please, continue," is all I can get out between my clenched teeth.

"So…when our oldest sister was born, Mother was allowed five minutes with her before she was taken from her, and he had the baby killed. Mother carried another daughter for her second pregnancy, three years later. You were her third attempt at bearing an heir for Avram. She was so ecstatic when you were born, and she was allowed to keep you. She refused a nanny and never let you out of her sight, always in fear that he would change his mind and take you from her."

I hadn't realized I'd begun to shed tears while Runa spoke until Leera accepted a box of tissues from Matilda and handed me the box after taking two for herself. I kept my mouth shut, allowing her to continue her painful monologue.

"She was also happy to have you as an only child, but Avram wanted more children and demanded she be a 'good mate' and 'do her duty.' He was an awful, vile mate and never deserved to be blessed by the goddess. What he didn't tell her was that he didn't want more children; he wanted more sons. When she became with child again, he wasn't happy with her. He acted as though he didn't care at all, and when she pressed him, he finally admitted that he would never accept a female heir. It destroyed her. To be told she would never be allowed to raise a daughter, and any she conceived wouldn't be allowed to live. She fell into a deep depression. He continued to berate her, and you continued to grow. You were everything to her," she chokes but waves her hand as to say, "I'm okay, give me a minute."

"She was forced to give up two daughters after you and began avoiding pregnancies at all cost, but he had forbidden the healers from giving her a tonic—"

"I'm sorry, what's a tonic?" my sweet little mate asks with a sniffle.

I answer gently, "It's what humans call birth control. It prevents pregnancy."

Leera nods and climbs back into my lap, holding onto me tightly.

"When you were, I think it was twelve years old, she got pregnant with me. As soon as she was aware, she finally confided in the queen what had been happening. The queen was her best friend, but they kept their friendship as private as they could because of him. The queen was appalled and ordered that her most trusted healer attend to her. They made up a story that she had fainted and taken a fall and needed round-the-clock care and ordered that only this healer was allowed to care for her. Avram was furious but settled when he began to test the healer, and she had gained his trust under the direction of the queen. When he was confident that he would get his way, he approached the healer with the same proposition as the old one…I'm gonna grab another coffee if that's okay?" She pauses as she rises to her feet.

"I think we could all use a break," I suggest as I rise myself. I don't want coffee, though; I'm headed to my office for my Zabellan whiskey that I keep on hand for when I need it. I don't have to go that far, though. Our sweet Matilda has already gotten it out for me and laid glasses and ice on the counter.

She smiles sweetly at me and opens her arms wide. I'm a few steps from her and actually in need of one of her hugs when Benny dashes in front of me and into her arms, stealing my hug. I growl, and the bastard gloats about it, but Matilda is too sweet to turn anyone away, so she finishes hugging him and calls me over.

"Come here, dear," she coos in that only-her voice, "I know it's a lot, but you're doing great. Keep listening. She needs to get this poisonous secret off her heart as much as you need to hear it."

"Yes, ma'am."

She pours me only 2 fingers of whiskey over a large cylindrical ice cube.

Come get some whiskey if you want it before I have her put it away. Someone tell Khaos, I tell my men. They each take a small glass and head back to the living room.

"I wasn't sure if you drank but you're welcome to have a glass of whiskey if you want also," I offer to Runa.

She shakes her head and responds, "Ha, no thanks, alcohol makes me more emotional." But she says it with a small smile, so I smile back.

When we're all settled back into our relative seats, Runa remains standing and begins pacing, "It helps me get my nervous energy out if I can move while I talk, please, just bear with me… where was I…oh, yeah, okay, so, he offered the healer the same proposition. A large sum of money in return for getting rid of the baby. She accepted the money and set it aside. When I was born, I was the first daughter that Mother had ever named because she couldn't bring herself to name the ones that would be sent back to the Goddess. She named me and spent ten minutes with me. The healer lied and told him there were complications from delivery that required additional care before she could take care of me. She then sedated me and got me out of the house and didn't stop running with me until she'd left Zabella. Once she got to the human realms, she paid for a lone werewolf family to care for me until I matured and could find my own way. They were kind and took amazing care of me, but there was no love. When the healer came back when I was of age and ready to head out on my own, she told me everything. Including that Mother didn't kill herself or die of sickness…he fucking killed her because she refused to bear anymore children for him—"

The growl that's ripped from my body is all my wolf. He's threatening to rip through my skin without warning. All I can see is red. All I can feel is blind rage.

Not only did this worthless creature kill my first mate and unborn child, but he murdered my mother because she refused to watch any more of her children die, and then he kidnapped Leera and would have killed her if we didn't find her.

"It's okay, Roman, let it out. We can take a break and go for a run?" Leera suggests calmly with tears in her eyes, but all I can do is nod before my wolf surges through my skin, shredding my clothes, and toppling over our large couch, thankful everyone was able to hop off in time.

"I'm here." Leera places her hand on my head and just holds it there while I focus on my breathing. "Okay, Big Guy, let's go run."

She dashes into the kitchen, crouching behind the cabinets, and I realize she's taking her clothes off so they're not shredded like mine. A moment later her beautiful silver wolf emerges and rushes back towards me. She nuzzles beneath my chin, rubbing her body against mine, then away from me, looking back over her shoulder and ticking her head for me to follow her.

7

Leera

Seeing my massive, strong-as-fuck, hockey-playing werewolf boyfriend hurt is crippling. Having to be the strong one while he gets through this isn't hard at all, though. Knowing how it feels to learn things about your own life, I'm just glad I can be there for him and make sure he learns to lean on the people that care about him.

Walking out of their massive townhouse in my wolf's body felt weird, but now I understand them living more secluded against a wooded area. We take off towards the forest, thinning with the change in seasons. I notice I'm seeing Khaos' black wolf for the first time. His black wolf is different than Slate's. Where Slate is a true deep black, a little shorter and wider, thick with muscle, Khaos' wolf's fur is so black it looks blue in the sunlight, and he's built taller and leaner. If I had to guess, his wolf could be underestimated, but I have no doubt he's just as strong, if not stronger than most.

The final wolf I'm unfamiliar with must be Runa. She's smaller than the guys but bigger than me. She's timid, staying close to Khaos, so I take the moment to break away from Roman for a moment, after a nuzzle, of course. Her wolf has a stunning, unique coat. At first glance, you'd only see dark charcoal-colored fur, but a closer look shows the much lighter, almost white undercoat. I wag my tail and try my best to look like I'm smiling as I approach. I want her to feel welcome, and maybe we can even be friends. I run around her and Khaos and back to Roman, knocking his hips with mine when I catch back up. When I look back at her, the rest of the men are catching up with us, leaving the twins bringing up the rear.

We run through the wooded area and cornfields for a couple of hours until our wolves are panting and my soul feels lighter. Roman looks better too. I think he spent some of the time talking to his men through their mind-link that I'm still obnoxiously jealous of. I want to be able to communicate with him and my brothers. I need to remember to ask Roman how that can work with Khaos.

When we enter the garage, you can hear all of our nails click-clacking against the cement, and we're stopped by Miss Tilly. "You can all just stop right there. You're not all tracking dirty paws through the whole house." She chuckles and points to the piles of clothes laid out across the beds of the trucks and one of the cars. "Leera, dear, you can come over here," and she points to my clothes and a standing partition that I hope she didn't drag down here just for me.

I focus on returning to my human body and am still amazed as I watch my fur recede and my smooth, freckled skin return. I've barely gotten my clothes on when Roman sneaks up behind me and scoops me into his arms, eliciting a small squeal from my lungs. "Thank you," he mumbles into my neck.

"Always," I reassure him. "Now let's go finish this heavy discussion."

We all make our way back to the main floor and are greeted by a small lunch buffet spread across the kitchen island.

"Miss Tilly, you do too much!" I mock-scold her. I appreciate everything she does for us, but I don't want her to wear herself out. "Nonsense, I've been taking care of my boys for years. I wouldn't have it any other way," she simultaneously beams while putting me in my place.

Benny throws what looks like five turkey pinwheels in his mouth at once and squashes her in a giant hug with a muffled, "We'd be woft wifout you Miff Tiwy," causing us all to laugh. Of course, the men more huff than actually laugh, but you get the picture.

We stand around the kitchen, snacking and chatting with one another in one of the most relaxed conversations we've had in days, and it feels so good. We definitely need to be going for more runs if this is how it feels.

The peace is broken when Roman chooses to go ahead and continue the earlier discussion about where we all stand. "Why didn't you come to me?" he asks, his voice gravely and pained.

Runa gingerly sets down her glass of tea and meets his eyes. "I wanted to. So many times. But I couldn't be sure whether or not it was safe. I've watched your entire hockey career, and what I could of you, but I couldn't be sure you weren't just like him."

Roman growls, but she lifts a hand to stop him. "Let's turn the tables then. If you only knew what you could see from the outside, what would you have thought? A man who was raised by this monster. Who then rises within the ranks of the military and becomes the Commander of the King's Werewolf Army. But wait, there's more. He's betrothed to the King's advisor's daughter. The same man who went with the monster to obtain the prophecy. You hold no public grudges against your father. You only recently ended the engagement with India. You tell me, Roman, what would you think?"

I already know the answer because I can completely see her perspective as someone who also came from outside their ranks. He knows too because he hangs his head and lets out a strangled, "FUCK!"

"I'm not mad at you for doing what you had to do to get through that life. I'm not mad at you at all. I just couldn't risk it. No matter how many times I've wanted to just…die…" she chokes on a fresh sob, and growls erupt around the room. "I couldn't let her sacrifice mean nothing."

I can't hold back anymore. I dash across the kitchen and wrap her in a hug. I don't even know if she likes hugs, but anyone who has felt those feelings alone deserves a hug. She slowly returns the hug, wrapping her arms around my upper back as she's probably five inches taller than me. Once her arms have completely wrapped around me, the dam breaks, and this strong woman shatters into pieces. I hold her tighter as she cries against me. Slowly, my amazing new family joins me, one by one, starting with Miss Tilly, who joins us with an, "Oh, my sweet dears," while she pats our backs. Khaos and Roman come in simultaneously and crush us in a loving and comforting werewolf-sandwich-hug.

"Come on, everyone in!" Benny yells, dragging Slate and Andrei into the group hug.

The twins look apprehensive, but after a sideways glare from Roman, they also join the moment.

The men nearly immediately begin pulling away, but I have a

rule when it comes to hugs. I never stop hugging first. You never know how much someone needs it. So, I continue to hold on until I feel Runa begin to pull away, and our watery eyes meet each other's. "Roman, she gets to stay, right? She's been through so much, and now you two can get to know each other."

Roman's face softens as he smiles. "She can stay if she would like, but that's up to her and her Alpha." He nods towards Khaos.

"Wait. Before you decide completely, there's one other thing." Runa pulls her hands from mine to wring them together in front of her, eyes darting around the room.

I'm looking between Roman and Runa, his eyes narrowing in suspicion. "What is it?"

"You don't have to tell him if you don't want to," Dolos says, the edge in his voice startling me.

Runa shakes her head. "If I'm going to be getting to know my brother and creating a life here, I won't start it with half-truths or whatever his deal is…" She pauses, her cheeks turning pink. "The twins are my mates."

8
ROMAN

That was the absolute last thing I expected to leave her mouth, but also, now everything makes sense. "Is this what the fuck's been wrong with you two lately?" I ask, turning to the twins. The twins who don't look as happy as they should about having found their fated mate.

Dolos nods, but Eris looks to draw even deeper within himself.

We're all just standing here, but no one is saying anything.

"What the hell is going on? What's wrong with you?" I nearly roar, my irritation at their strange behavior peaking.

"Nothing," is all Eris grunts, and Dolos just shakes his head at him.

I point my finger at him. "Listen here, I don't know what crawled up your ass, or what your problem is, but you better figure it out," I bark.

"I can go," Runa says lightly with Leera by her side.

"You've done nothing wrong. Do you know why they're acting like this?" I ask her, trying to remember not to growl at her for something that isn't her fault.

Eris rises and begins to stomp out of the room, causing me to bark at him, "Sit your lousy-attitude-ass down," and he does.

Runa nods but continues, "They've apparently got some personal stuff they need to work through, and so do I…" she trails off, but I can hear the pain of rejection in her voice.

So help me Goddess, if my own men put my sister through that kind of pain, I will maul them myself. I know they always joked about never wanting a mate, but no one ever thought they were serious. "If that's how you two are going to be, then you don't deserve—"

"It's not like that," Dolos interrupts, now rising to his feet.

"Well, it's obviously like something, isn't it?" I cross my arms over my chest.

"Until I'm sure you can appreciate her and treat her the way she deserves, Runa is off limits—"

"Roman!" Leera and my sister shout in unison, both planting their hands on their hips. It surprises them, and they stop and turn to look at each other before smiling, in turn making me smile.

Leera approaches me. "Roman, honey, don't you think we should stay out of their business?" She looks around to our family.

I tilt my head to the side in mock contemplation before smiling at her and replying, "Nope," making sure to pop the "P" for a dramatic effect. "If they're going to treat their mate this way, who happens to be my little sister, then no. When they've buttoned up whatever their problem is, I'll consider it."

Leera shakes her head at me but doesn't push it further.

"You really don't have to do that. I can handle myself just fine. I have been for almost seven hundred years," Runa scolds me, also crossing her arms over her chest.

Again, I tilt my head back and forth as if weighing my thoughts. "While that may be the case, it never would have happened. I would have taken care of you, and that's what I'm going to do now. Those idiots will figure it out. They always do. But I'm not letting you deal with their bullshit in the meantime."

At that, Eris does stomp out of the room, grumbling all the way. Dolos is hot on his heels but does stop to look me in the eye. "He's got some shit he needs to work through," he vaguely explains before turning to Runa. "Roman's not wrong, you deserve the world, and I'll make sure you get it." He takes her hand and plants a soft kiss on her knuckles before taking off after his brother.

"Well…this is fun!" Khaos says to everyone and no one in particular.

"Has anyone else found their mate that I should know about?" I ask in jest as I scrub my hand down my face.

Benny approaches and wraps his arms around my shoulder, "Nah, Boss, I'm still all yours," and we all break into laughter, even Runa.

"Hey, are you okay?" Leera asks her, and my sister nods. "Yeah, it's…it's just been a lot."

Leera soothes her and begins to lead her towards our room. "I can only imagine. Did you know that I didn't even know I was a werewolf…"

I can hear their voices trailing off, and I hope those two become friends. It would seem that was everyone's cue that we've discussed everything we needed to for the time being. Everyone rises and heads in different directions, leaving Khaos and me in the living room.

Thankful that Matilda left it out, I make my way to the whiskey for a much larger glass.

"Don't you have practice later?" he laughs.

I hold the decanter in the air towards him, silently asking if he'd like some himself, and he nods.

I fill the glasses and return with them and plop back down onto the couch after handing Khaos his. "Yeah, I do, but I'll never get through it if I put everyone through a wall," I grumble, taking a generous gulp of the smooth Zabellan whiskey.

Khaos does the same and shakes his head. "Everything went from routine to complicated real fucking quick, didn't it?"

I don't even answer him. He knows. I raise my glass, and he brings his to meet mine, clinking them together.

9
Leera

The last few weeks have gone by in a comfortable and only slightly chaotic sort of monotony, all of us settling back into our routines. Sure, the world still feels like it's on fire as long as Roman's father and his counterparts walk free, but we can't put our entire lives on hold while we do what we can.

By we, I mean the men, mostly Slate. I don't know how that man can even see with the amount of time his face spends staring at a laptop or other electronic device.

He still hasn't found anything that leads us to where Avram is hiding out, and we can't exactly storm Zabella and take on the King's advisor without all the evidence, lost princess or not.

So, I've been getting all my schoolwork done between hockey games and practices. Most of the boring academic stuff is already completed for the semester, so I get to spend the majority of my time on my photojournalism assignments.

Nearly all of my assignments have featured the Predators, but we did have one recently that allowed me to choose a zoo-keeper to shadow at the Cleveland Zoo. Naturally, I requested the wolves, which turned out to be a group of six Mexican gray wolves. I got to feed them, clean up after them, and photograph them, of course.

My favorite part was the way they looked at me. They didn't lower their heads and watch me, like they did with the keepers. They kept their heads up, eyes locked on mine, with the occasional tilt to their head like they were trying to figure me out. My wolf perked up and was all excited over the change in scenery, and it was almost a struggle to convince her that we couldn't just shift and make new friends. I settled with letting a little of her energy out when one of the wolves was making eye contact with me again. I was surprised when she yipped at me, and her tail began to wag. The keepers were in awe that after that the wolves were following me around, and they even let me pet them. I decided that I would have to bring the guys to visit them one day as well.

Khaos had to return to his hockey team in Augusta since the season was still in full swing. He had slipped into our family surprisingly well for being Roman's lifelong rival. I think a lot of that comes from actually taking the time to understand each other without their fathers hanging over their shoulders.

Runa and I have become good friends, and when Zoey stayed over last weekend, the three of us were inseparable. It's hard keeping secrets from Zoey about everything going on in my life, so I'm glad I have another girl I can talk to, other than Miss Tilly, of course.

Tonight, the guys have a big home game against the Kansas City Warriors. I guess this is their next biggest division rival, after Khaos' team, of course. They're neck-and-neck in points; even though it's only December, the teams are already laser-focused on getting that home rink advantage in the playoffs. Well, most of the teams are laser-focused. It's not that the Predators aren't; it's just hard with everything we have going on. I've been trying to convince them to try and enjoy the game they loved so much before I came along, but it's still a work in progress.

I also finally talked Runa into joining me for the game tonight. Between the twins and the giant crowds, she's managed to avoid going so far. But I told her I'd be there with her the whole time, along with our guard, because I still can't go anywhere alone. After the interaction at the game with Khaos, I'm thankful for the extra layer of protection.

The new guard Roman has on standby is a large and terrifyingly beautiful woman that goes by Fran. Not Franny, not Francine, not Frankie, just Fran. I know because I asked. She doesn't really talk or smile or do anything but watch. Everything. Which again I appreciate, but she's so intimidating. I'm pretty sure she could bench press Benny, which would be really fun to watch. I'm glad I'll have Runa with me tonight so I can talk to someone who talks back.

The men are all at their pregame meeting, so it's just us girls at the house. I talked Runa and Miss Tilly into watching Twilight with me, and watching them watch the movie has been almost more fun than watching it with Roman.

"Vampires that sparkle?" Runa snorts. "You've got to be shitting me. I wonder how they feel about this monstrosity," she wheezes, doubled over in laughter. Her laugh is the contagious kind where I could have no idea why she was laughing, but if she's laughing, I'm laughing. And, apparently, so is Miss Tilly.

When we all recover from our ten-minute fit of laughter, my mind returns to me and registers what she's just said. "Wait, vampires are real too?" I don't know why I'm surprised, but the guys hadn't said it so directly, so I hadn't given it any more thought.

Runa's head ticks to the left when she looks at me. "Really? I thought Roman caught you up on everything you'd been missing?"

I just shrug, because as usual, I don't know how much I don't know.

"Yes, vampires are also real, but they're so much different than the movies. Like, they obviously do not sparkle," she scoffs, but I can tell she's trying not to erupt into another fit of laughter. "They do prefer less sunny areas, but only because it's more comfortable. They can be in the sun now, thanks to a tonic they developed with the white witches about a millennia ago, but the stronger UV rays still make them uncomfortable. One I met explained that it feels like wearing a wool bodysuit."

"Oof, that does sound awful. What other mythical things are real?" I ask, sipping on a passion fruit green tea from the café we had lunch delivered from.

"All of them," she says with too much seriousness. I start to laugh, but she gives me that head-tilt look again, and I realize she's serious.

Setting my cup down on the coffee table, I ask, "Wait, really? What about…dragons?"

She nods her head, slightly bobbing it left to right like she's weighing how to explain herself. "Yes and no. The—"

"What do you mean, yes and no?" I laugh.

"Well, it depends who you ask. If you ask more direct people who stop at what they're told, like my brother, he would probably say they used to exist, but I believe they're still out there."

I nod my head, understanding what she means. "So, like, with people who believe in aliens and angels? Some believe, and others are firm in their stance that some things just aren't possible."

"Exactly like that. They are, or were, shifters, you know? Dragons. I think they just got tired of being demonized for their beast forms and decided it was easier to disappear. When you're raised being told how impossible something is, it's easier to just remain a secret…" Her voice lowers as darker times flood her features.

Leaning forward, I take her hand in mine. "You're not there anymore, and you never have to go back. That place in your mind isn't needed anymore. Fuck your father—not literally because eww—but you know what I mean. Don't let him shadow you. I'm not," I finish, sitting taller and trying to sound braver than I am.

Runa gives me a weak smile and nods. I don't push her, and we return to watching the movie while she keeps pointing out the cringey moments everyone knows and loves.

Miss Tilly just watches us, taking everything in and not interjecting. I think it's killing her to sit still and watch the movie with us, but it's good for her to rest. I've never seen someone constantly need to be doing something the way she does.

The men arrive home just before the ending credits start rolling, and as soon as I hear the door open, at least two of them groan before Benny laughs. "Why are you torturing them with that mess?"

"It's been very educational." Runa tries to keep a straight face and hold in her laughter, but it ends up just making her release a raspberry sound. All laughter is forgotten when Eris comes through with that new constant nasty look on his face. Runa folds in on herself, sinking into the safe embrace of the couch. Unluckily for Eris, Dolos and Roman see it at the same time and stomp after him before slamming a door, and I can only barely hear the rumbles of their shouting.

Returning my attention to Runa, I say, "Hey, I'm sorry. It'll be okay eventually."

She nods, but it's one of those nods you give to someone just to be nice and hope they'll shut up. So I do. Shut up, I mean. We sit on the couch and cozy up in our blankets, ready to watch New Moon until it's time to get ready.

10
ROMAN

I've barely latched the door shut when Dolos rams into Eris like a freight train. "What the actual fuck is wrong with you?" he shouts, completely and totally exasperated by his twin. "Like, I knew some shit was bothering you, so I kept covering, but this is getting fucking ridiculous. Can't you feel how you're hurting her?!" Dolos looks out of his mind with worry. Likely for both his brother and his mate.

Eris slaps Dolos' arms away and shoves him back. "Go! Take care of her. Make her happy. All that shit. I. Can't."

"Why?" I demand.

"You two won't get it. Just back off and—"

"You're not rejecting our fucking mate, you asshole. Why the fuck would you even consider that?" Dolos shuts him down.

I've never seen these two like this, and we've been together since the beginning. They can be serious when the situation has called for it, more like a mask than actually taking something se-riously, but I've never seen Eris this serious and down on himself like this. I've never seen Dolos this devastated. "Will someone just tell me what the fuck is going on before I make you?" I level them both with a stare that says I'm serious, but it's apparently not as good as I once thought.

"You wouldn't," Eris scoffs, and I see red.

"I absolutely will if you force my hand. What the fuck is wrong with you?"

Dolos shuffles his feet and crosses his arms over his chest. "There are bits of our past we haven't shared. Shit we grew up with. I mean, yeah, the shit sucks, but it wasn't so bad that I wouldn't accept my mate…That's what's pissing me off; I don't know what his deal is…"

"Like I fucking said, you two won't get it, and I'm not fucking talking about it. Use your Alpha shit on me if you want, but if you do…I'm going to need some time away…I might anyways."

Eris doesn't even stop to look at Dolos and me as he stomps out of the room, slamming the door and leaving us in shock.

It takes us a minute to gather our bearings. "What the fuck just happened?" I growl.

"I'd really fucking like to know." Dolos stares at the door like he can see his brother through it. "I know he hated our parents and went through some shit on some of our missions, but none of it explains the way he's acting."

I sit and allow everything that just happened to take root in my mind. "Whatever he's going through has to be enough that he's willing to go through an unimaginable amount of pain by avoiding your mate. While having the same mate might be part of it, it's definitely not all of it."

Dolos only nods.

"New plan of action. We're going to have to back off. I don't want to force him to deal with whatever demons are haunting him if they're going to drive him away from us. You're going to continue to get to know Runa and soothe her worries the best you can. We'll give Eris time while we deal with the rest of the shit we've got going on and hope that by the time we've reached a place where we can tackle whatever's going on, he'll be ready to move forward. I'm sorry, but I think it's best that you don't complete your mate bond without your brother. I don't think that would be a good idea."

Again, Dolos just nods, clearly not expecting his brother's outburst.

"Go try to calm him down. We've still got a game to play."

The guys left a while ago to get ready for the game, so it's just Runa and me waiting for Fran to pick us up for the game. It took a bit of convincing, but I was finally able to cheer Runa up and get her to dress up with me for the game.

We didn't even finish the movie earlier. Eris blew out of the room the guys were in like a bomb waiting to go off. We tried to ignore him, but I could feel the pain radiating off of Runa, and I hated it. Roman came out a few minutes later, kissed me on the forehead, and told us it would be okay. Dolos was the last to come in the room, looking completely defeated until the door clicked shut and Runa looked over at him. It was like watching those cute lovesick cartoons as a natural smile bloomed on his face.

"Sorry for interrupting your movie, ladies," he apologized dramatically, causing me to giggle. Runa was not as convinced. She turned her head away, lifting her chin in defiance, and it looked like he'd been struck.

I felt like I was impeding and had tried to slowly scoot off the couch to sneak away, but Runa latched onto my hand like a lifeline, her eyes begging me to stay. So I did, no matter how awkward I felt to encroach on something that had the potential to become a "moment" if they'd only let it.

Dolos approached cautiously and knelt in front of her, slowly taking her other hand in his, effectively gaining her attention. "I truly am sorry this hasn't gone the way it should. Please don't give up on us, on him." He kissed her knuckles sweetly, rose to his feet, and walked away, not waiting for a response.

When he was out of sight, Runa released a deep sigh and shook her head. "All right, let's get ready for this game then," she said with a small smile on her face.

When we started getting ready, and I pulled out Roman's jersey, a wistful look briefly crossed her face, but I didn't want her thinking about all of that tonight, so I asked Benny for one of his jerseys. He was all too excited to let us borrow one, like I'm missing a great big joke, but at least that was taken care of. Instead of having to decide if she wanted to wear Eris' number one or Dolos' number two, she would wear Benny's number thirty-two.

She's decided to go with a pair of dark-wash jeggings and combat boots, while I chose fleece-lined, nude leggings and a pleated skirt that's only a couple inches longer than Roman's jersey I'm wearing.

She straightened her dark locks and is rocking a dark smoky-eye, while I curled my silver hair and went with a bright and glittery makeup look.

We chatted and took turns playing our favorite songs while we got ready together in mine and Roman's bathroom. It was fun, but it made me miss Zoey, so I made a mental note to invite her to more hockey games with us.

Fran finally pulls up, sans smile, and gracefully rushes out of the driver's seat to come around the car and open the door to the back seat for us. I scoot in first as quickly as I can so that Runa can join me. "Have you been to *any* hockey games before?" I ask as we settle in for the short drive to the arena.

"Only if a bunch of pack wolves playing on a frozen lake counts," she laughs.

I clap my hands. "Ohhh this is going to be so much fun! Wait until you see the seats Roman got us."

We pull up to the arena, and Fran parks underneath the closest visible security camera. Runa and I adjust our clothing as we hop out of the car. When Fran makes it around the car to us, Runa looks up at the behemoth arena in awe.

There are people everywhere pulling into the parking lot and flooding through the large glass doors. I still get such a rush walking into this building after my earlier encounters here. This is where it all started, after all.

Runa and I walk hand-in-hand with Fran following closely behind us on full alert. We walk past all the little shops and food vendors, stopping to grab a few little souvenirs on the way. "We don't have to grab food because we have a concierge to serve us at our seats," I say with a smile when I see her checking out all the yummy dinner options.

We finish ogling all the things we can spend money on and head to find our seats. The cold air splashes across our skin, and I'm smiling so big it almost hurts.

"Whoa," she breathes as she takes it all in.

This place is truly massive. It's not even full yet, but there are literally people everywhere. With our hands still linked, I pull us all the way down to the ice where the guys are doing those wonderful warm-up drills that made it to the internet and took the world by storm. I'm watching Roman stretch his hips when he must notice we're here because he snaps his face in my direction and stretches more dramatically, causing me to hide my face in my hands so no one can see how hard I'm blushing.

Runa snickers, but she's watching the twins just as intently. Dolos winks at her with a dazzling smile, while Eris continues to pretend she doesn't exist, causing Dolos to stop his stretches, kicking his leg and spraying Eris with ice. When she turns to me, Dolos notices she's wearing Benny's jersey and lunges for him while Benny laughs like an idiot. They roll around on the ice for a minute before Coach yells at them to "knock it the fuck off" before he benches them.

When they come up from the ice, Benny's still smiling like a crazy person. Dolos makes eye contact with Runa, pointing to his jersey, then back to her. She dramatically rolls her eyes and shrugs like she doesn't know why he's mad before turning her back on him completely to walk with me to our seats.

We plop down in a fit of giggles and order an obnoxious amount of food when the concierge stops by and asks us for our order. They arrive with our refreshments just as the lights dim, the music is turned up, and the pregame show begins.

12
ROMAN

The game starts like any other, but it quickly escalates into mayhem. You'd think we were playing the Vultures with the level of intensity the Warriors came out with tonight. I know we're a rival, but something just feels off. Both teams have had multiple people in and out of the penalty box for both periods so far.

The Warriors have the puck, they're down by one, and they're pushing towards the goal. Their captain lines up his shot, but Slate is ready and knocks the shot away. Dolos rushes to dig the puck out of the corner, but he doesn't reach the puck. Two Warriors fly out of nowhere, charging in with their heads lowered, and both smash into Dolos' ribs. The sound of them cracking echoes through the pack bond, sending a ripple of pain through all of us. The entire crowd gasps as one and rises to their feet.

If I thought this game was mayhem before, it's an absolute disaster now. Dolos is crumpled on the ice, and I'm bolting towards him. Eris, however, has lost all control. He's ripped his helmet off, and any Warrior player that comes anywhere near him instantly regrets it. He's yanking their helmets off and throwing his fists so hard into their faces that there are teeth being lost tonight. Benny tries to pull him off and calm him, but it's like he can't hear him or anyone for that matter.

When I reach Dolos, he's still conscious but unable to move due to his fractured ribs. He's taking staggered and shallow breaths to avoid the sharp pains that come from attempting to take in too much air at once. Unfortunately, this isn't the first time we've encountered these injuries; it's just been a very long time.

The crowd is roaring now; fans of both teams still on their feet, screaming and banging their fists on the glass barriers.

I look back up to check on Eris, and the refs are trying to pull him off of one of the men who hit his brother, but they're not making any real progress. It looks like all that pent-up shit he won't deal with finally took over. *Eris, get your shit together and calm down.* He doesn't have his mental shields up, so I know he heard me, but he doesn't even flinch at my words.

I see a flash of silver pass by the glass behind Eris, and a spark of fear tries to take root until I notice she's following Runa, and they're both being followed by Fran.

Runa bangs on the plexiglass barrier with one closed fist, raises her other hand to her mouth to release a loud whistle, and yells, "MARZOLLI!"

He flinches and stills, slowly turning his head.

She yells again, pointing at Eris then Dolos, "Eris! Knock it off, he's going to be fine!"

Leera's brows are creased in worry as her eyes dart to where I'm kneeling beside Dolos and where Eris still has the nearly unconscious Warrior by his jersey, shrugging off the players and refs who are still trying to stop him.

Eris' shoulders drop like he's finally snapped out of the

rage-induced trance he was drowning in, and he slowly releases the Warriors player to sink to the ice. The refs get ahold of him, and he stops fighting, letting them drag him off the ice where he's granted a misconduct penalty and ejected from the game.

After the medical team is able to get Dolos off the ice and into the locker rooms where the healers will see to him, the game is able to resume with the two players that hit Dolos also receiving misconduct penalties, but they just have ten minutes in the penalty boxes, giving us ten minutes of power play to make sure we take this game. Then we're going to figure out what the fuck the weird energy was about tonight.

Our post-game meeting and interviews felt like they dragged on forever. The second I'm able, I bolt away to find my little mate. When I approach, she and my sister have their heads tucked together in conversation. "I hope I'm not interrupting," I say with intentional intensity, causing them both to startle. I chuckle, but they both swat at me, and Leera crosses her arms in front of her chest, making me nearly groan out loud.

"How's Dolos?" the girls ask in unison.

"He'll be fine. He has one fractured rib, but it should be healed up by morning."

They both release a sigh of relief.

"Runa, he'd probably like it if you rode home with him. Give him a mental boost, ya know?" I suggest calmly.

She nods, wringing her hands together as she moves to leave, but not before Leera stops her and wraps her in a tight hug. We watch Runa catch up to where they're helping Dolos down the tunnel to the back exit of the arena. When she's caught up and in good hands, Leera turns to me and jumps into my arms, wrapping her legs around my waist and peppering my face with kisses between her words, "I don't like when there are big fights. I don't like worrying about you guys." She stops and looks me in the eyes, her icy-blue ones melting into calmness. "I'm glad it wasn't you this time. Does that make me a bad person?"

I squeeze my arms around her tighter. "Not at all. We understand. I'm glad you and Fran were with Runa for that…Also…did you two feel anything weird from the stands?" I ask cautiously, trying not to induce an anxiety-riddled panic attack.

She visibly thinks for a moment. "I don't think so…I mean, not really. Like the fans all felt normal, but the game definitely seemed rough. Like there was more than just playoff points on the line."

I nod to myself for a moment. "I was thinking the same thing. There was a weird energy on the ice tonight, and I want to figure out why."

Leera and I are the last ones to make it home. I carry her in and plop her cute little ass on the top of the long kitchen island we tend to gather at. "Slate, I want you to dig into the Warriors team; give me everything you can find. Something felt off at that game tonight."

"Ya think, Boss? They were nearly rabid. I don't know how they weren't shifting left and right with the way they were acting," Benny adds.

I walk over to the couch where Dolos is resting, propped up

by probably two dozen pillows, with Runa by his side, and Eris across the room sitting in a chair, just watching them. "How're you holding up?"

Dolos gives me an ornery grin and says, "Right as rain. I'm sure I'm fine, but someone has decided I'm couch-bound until morning," he finishes, his eyes darting towards my sister, who isn't looking at me.

"Sounds like a good plan to be sure." I pat him on his shoulder, and he winces a bit, telling me Runa was right and that he needs to allow himself to rest.

Andrei comes walking in from down the hall with a letter in his hand. "People still write letters?" I ask.

He doesn't immediately look up. "We do when we're communicating between the realms and don't want our digital information to be tracked," he snaps back before immediately adding, "Shit, I'm sorry. I reached out to some of my contacts I trust to see if anyone had noticed strange movement with Avram or Boian… Nothing major, though. Apparently, Boian has been a little scarce lately, but nothing more. Avram has been in and out of the realm a little more than usual, but he keeps losing his tails."

Not what we wanted to hear, but it's something. I nod to Andrei, and he plops onto one of the barstools near Leera, and they start chatting as I walk over to Slate and his laptop. "I have an uncomfortable hunch. See if anyone on the Warriors team has any connections to my father, the advisor, or dark witches."

Slate nods and begins typing, losing himself in the information on his screen. Benny's rummaging through the refrigerator when he pops his head out, mouth full, and mutters, "How wa gowwa figwa out da pwaphucy?"

Leera throws her head back and laughs, and the sound feels

like magic. "What on Earth did you just say?"

I chuckle with her and roll my eyes, translating his gibberish, "He asked how we're going to figure out the prophecy. Don't worry, give it a couple hundred years, and you'll be able to understand him too." And the rest of the room laughs along with us.

When we've all stopped laughing, Leera speaks up, "I actually had an idea that might help."

Everyone in the room perks up to pay attention. "I'm listening," I offer suspiciously because if she thinks she's doing anything that would even remotely put her in danger, it's not fucking happening.

She hops off the counter and takes the few steps it takes to reach me, wrapping her arms around me, tilting her head back to look me in the eyes with her sweet smile on her face. "Calm down, Big Guy, I was just going to suggest seeing if Prof—Willa wants to meet for coffee or something, and we could talk to her and see if she knows how we can learn about the prophecy."

"That's…that's actually a great idea."

"Wow, Roman." She jabs me in my chest. "Don't sound so surprised that I could have a good idea." She pouts, crossing her arms.

I cough out a small laugh. "That's most definitely not how I meant that. I only meant that I should have thought of it."

She gives me the side-eye. "Nice cover."

I scoop her into my arms and toss her gently over my shoulder. "That's enough business for the day. Goodnight, everyone! Say goodnight, darling."

"Roman! Put! Me! Down!" she squeals while playfully beating her tiny fists on my back before giving up in a heap of defeat and huffing, "Goodnight, guys."

While I was initially surprised and a bit embarrassed at the way Roman tossed me over his shoulder, my embarrassment quickly melted into need. It looks like I can add "being man-handled" to the list of things that he does that make my panties wet…which he's also taken notice of. I know because I hear him take in a large breath through his nose, followed by a deliciously low growl that reverberates through my core.

"Does my sweet little mate like to be thrown around?" he taunts, his voice dripping with promise.

I try to maintain my cool, but my voice comes out too breathy when I respond, "I don't know what you're talking about," I lie to both of us.

My wolf scoffs at me, and Roman chuckles in an obnoxiously sexy way.

Why is everything he does such a turn-on? It's getting—

My thoughts are cut off when he heaves my small body back over his shoulder, lightly dropping me on the plush bedding. He looms over me with that wickedly delightful look in his eyes. I don't know how long I just drink him in. Starting with his sandy hair, moving to his eyes—one blue, one green—both absolutely devastating, but my view is impeded by him removing his shirt. *I suppose that was worth the brief distraction.* His strong jaw and muscled shoulders make the most famous sculptures around the world look like wimps, and that's before you get to his pecs and chiseled abs leading straight to that glorious V muscle, drawing me in to exactly where I want to go.

My mouth waters at the thought, so I make my move and crawl over to him. "And what do you think you're doing?" he asks with his eyes shining with love and burning for me.

"I find I'm famished and only craving one thing," I say with a smile as I look into his eyes while unclasping his jeans, granting me access to what I want. I lower his boxers and wrap my hand around him. He's smooth as silk and hard as steel, and he's all mine.

I carefully trace the veins, causing him to jerk in my grasp. Making eye contact once more, I slowly lean in, licking him completely from bottom to tip. Once I've done that a few times and his hand snakes gently into my hair, holding my head, I lower my mouth completely over the tip.

"Fuck," he breathes, and I can feel my heartbeat between my legs.

I groan around him, and his hips jerk slightly. I begin moving to my own rhythm, taking him as far as I comfortably can, swirling my tongue around, and then sucking hard on the way back up while he curses and moans, his grip on my hair tightening ever so slightly. It's enough that he has my attention without an ounce of pain, and when my core clenches at the action, I add that to my list of things that turn me on and tuck them away for later.

All of a sudden, Roman is quite literally yanking me off his dick, leaving my mouth with a popping sound. "All right, Princess, that's enough of that. You come first. Always."

Well, who am I to argue with that?

He begins pulling away all the layers I was wearing at the game, starting with my jersey, when he growls, "One day I'll fuck you wearing just my jersey. Would you like that?"

All I can do is nod while my mouth waters at the thought of him finally marking me, and a shiver ripples through my body. I lean back, allowing him to pull off my skirt and leggings, leaving me in the matching maroon set of lingerie I managed to hide from him until the game tonight. He takes a step back and takes me in; there's need and love burning in his gaze when I start to squirm. "Roman," I plead.

He removes his pants from his ankles torturously slow, knowing I'm watching his every move before he crawls over me on the bed and crashes his lips to mine. I'll never get used to the electricity pinging through my body from his touch. I match the need and urgency in his kiss, arching my body into his, moaning into his lips. He finally pulls away, and his nearly glowing gaze finds mine as he moves in and begins kissing behind my ear. One hand is barely pinching my nipple, while the other traces the lightest circles around my clit. His mouth finally makes it to my other breast, sucking my other nipple into his mouth and gently nipping at the little bud.

I cry out at all the glorious sensations rippling through my body. It's like each part of my body is an instrument that only he knows how to play, and it's causing an entire symphony in my very bloodstream. It continues to crescendo and staccato through every fiber of my being while I pant and praise his name. "More,"

I beg, but he shocks my entire system when he pulls away completely. "Wh-what are you doing?" I whimper.

"Oh, don't worry, I'm not done with you yet, my little miracle." He leans down and leaves open-mouthed kisses on the inside of my thigh, and I'm not prepared for the intensity of that simple act. I'm also not prepared as he moves higher and sucks on the tender skin on the highest point of my inner thigh.

My back arches off the bed, hard. "Please, Roman!"

His mouth finally, and entirely too lightly, reaches the sweet bundle of nerves, and my eyes slam shut at the force of how close I am to falling off that wonderful cliff. I'm focused entirely on the beautifully filthy things his mouth is doing when he slides his fingers into my core and my body catches fire. He adds a second finger and slides them in until he reaches my resistance and holds them there while he devours me.

"Oh…G-God…Please, don't stop," I plead as I feel the swell of pleasure filling me.

At my words, his other hand climbs my body and latches onto one of my nipples, essentially flinging me into the abyss, screaming his name.

It always feels like an out-of-body experience when he makes me come, and I have to wonder if everyone feels this way. My body feels like all my bones have been dissolved and no longer hold any form of structural integrity.

When I fully come back to my body, I'm nearly ready to go again at the sight beside me. Roman is sitting, his back leaning against the headboard, stroking himself, ever so slowly.

I roll over onto my stomach between his legs. "Why don't you let me take care of that?" I ask, trying my best to be sultry and hoping I'm doing it right.

He smiles at me and crooks his finger, beckoning me closer. I oblige and move so that I'm just in front of him, close enough that I stick my tongue out and lick the end of his dick that he's still slowly stroking.

"When will I have all of you?" I accidentally think out loud, and he stops for a moment.

"I've only been trying to make sure you were ready and that it was perfect," he swears, lightly trailing his fingers across my skin.

I lean into him and sigh. "I am definitely ready," I pout.

He smiles. "I know, Leera. That's why I've been working on what I hope is the perfect night." It's really not fair that he's that fucking gorgeous when he smiles that I can't even be irritated with him.

I roll my eyes and climb into his lap, positioning myself just over his hardened length. "A plan, huh?" I taunt while I begin to grind myself against him. His head falls back while he breathes a staggered, "yes." I continue grinding on him, that now-familiar feeling rising within me while I watch my movements impact this strong, immortal man, and it drives me to move faster.

"Oh, fuck," we groan in unison, causing me to giggle.

Looking down to watch where our bodies touch, ready for more, I continue to rock my hips until his large hands clamp down on my hips and my head flies up to meet his eyes. In them I find nothing but burning need when he growls, "My turn."

He starts slowly, moving at just the right angle to rub himself against my clit without being inside of me. Once he's happy with his rhythm, he speeds up as well until his movements become erratic, and when I move in to kiss him, he pulls away, and I notice his teeth have lengthened, which tells me not to push it because it's taking all of his willpower not to mark me now incompletely.

The sight is my undoing, and the orgasm barrels through my body before I even know what's happening, Roman right behind me, roaring his release.

I fall into a heap of flesh against his chest. My heart clenches a little that I still didn't get my way and get to experience making love to my mate, but I know it's because he's doing right by me.

Maybe I put too much pressure on waiting. I snort to myself before sleep pulls me under.

The next day starts like most; the guys are off to their day-after-game-day meeting to watch the film from the game. They study their errors and opportunities, but this time the men will also be studying the Warriors to see if there's any indications about what their problems were at the game.

My plan for the day is also in motion. I texted Willa after the guys left and asked if she was available to meet for coffee or something so that we could talk. I'm hoping she knows something about prophecies so that, for once, there's a way that I'm able to help. I loathe feeling useless.

I'm pulled out of my self-directed angry thoughts by the ping of my phone.

Willa

Hey Leera! I'd love to meet up. My last class today is over in a couple hours. Want to meet at Cool Beans around 1pm?

I do have an appointment in the early evening but we should have plenty of time.

> Sounds perfect. See you there!

I can successfully mark that off my to-do list.

> Hey Fran–sorry to bother you but could you take me to Cool Beans so I get there at 1 and then not be super shadowy and uncomfortable and weird for a little bit?

> Like maybe wait outside?

> I just need to have an important conversation and you kinda draw attention

Shit, that sounded mean.

Fran

> Requesting approval now.

Excuse me? I don't-freaking-think so.

> Since when does Fran have to approve picking me up? Roman this had better not be a new thing.

Roman

> I'm assuming it was because I hadn't given her a heads up. Sorry Princess, it's not a requirement, she's just being thorough for your safety.

> I love you.

> Yea yea I love you too you overbearing grumpy wolf.

I hope he gets in trouble for not paying attention during the film review, I huff to myself.

With my plan in motion, I write a note for Runa, letting her know that I'm getting ready to leave and will be back later. I haven't seen her this morning since the debacle with the twins last night. I don't know what Eris' problem is, but I hope he figures it out. For all of our sakes.

Surprisingly, Fran is dressed in more normal clothing today, forgoing her usual all-black tactical vibes. She even made herself comfortable on the bench outside Cool Beans after watching me enter, without a short lecture about why she should be within arm's reach of me or something.

When the door closes behind me and takes the cool air with it, I consider that I might have overdressed for the chill as I quickly start warming up. I'm wearing a fuzzy baby-powder-pink sweater with slits up the sides, light gray fleece-lined leggings, and my black combat boots. My hair is tied up in a slick back ponytail with a puffy white scary wrapped around my neck.

Fate pulling me to Roman has to be why I decided to go to college in freaking Ohio. I hate the cold. Always have. My parents luckily didn't have many cold-weather assignments throughout my life. I remember becoming immensely thankful for that when we took the trip to Finland. They were asked to photograph one of those new destination resorts with the glass igloos and northern lights. Was it one of the single most beautiful things I'd ever seen in my entire life? Abso-fucking-lutely. Is it one of my favorite pictures of us as a family that's now resting on my bedside table at home? Yup. But it was so cold I felt like my bones were frozen and my brain couldn't even work. I'm just not hardwired that way, apparently.

Now that I think about it, I wonder if it was because of my wolf being suppressed because, I just realized, I wasn't cold at the full moon thingy at the pack lands recently when I would have normally been freezing. I've always been easily chilled.

I tuck that thought away for later when Willa rises from a table near the window—*Fran will love this*—to hug me.

"Leera! It's so good to see you again. How is everything? Oh, here, I took the opportunity to grab us both some coffee. I assumed you liked yours sweet, but let me know if I'm wrong, and I'll grab you something else." She radiates warmth and happiness, and I couldn't contain the smile on my face if I wanted to.

I hug her fiercely. "You didn't have to do that, but thank you! I do love my coffee very sweet," I beam at her as we settle into our seats, and I continue, "Mostly really great, but the bad is still braided in there, unfortunately."

She's sipping her coffee when I say that, and her brows scrunch together as she sets her deep green Cool Beans mug down on the table. "How much more bad? How bad?"

Allowing myself a nice long sip of my coffee, I gather myself and tell her absolutely everything that's happened since I last saw her. I had intended to not be quite so blunt about everything, but she's the only person that I feel I can really talk to and completely be myself with. Runa doesn't want to hear about the mushy stuff with Roman and me. Zoey can't know anything about the rest of my world. So, I let it all out. Every hairy detail. Though a sentence or two into my word-vomit, Willa did hold up a hand for me to pause while she mumbled a little to herself. Then she explained that she had placed a sound barrier around us so that our conversation would be completely private.

By the time I was finished, she just stared at me for a moment, obviously still processing everything, so I went ahead and threw in, "Soooo, that's the reason I wanted to meet up. I needed to get all that off my chest, but I—er, we—were hoping you knew something about how we could find out what that prophecy was."

She nods, more to herself, and finishes off her coffee, then carefully sets it down with both hands, watching it all the way, before slowly bringing her eyes back up to mine. "Before we go any further, are you okay?"

An unexpected laugh escapes me. "I mean, yeah, I think so. I kind of have to be." I keep on laughing nervously. She leans across the table, taking my small pale, hand in her warm, motherly, dark one, and softly rubs her thumb against my skin. "No, you don't, Leera. It's okay to not be okay. You know that, don't you?"

I intend to nod, but, instead, my head takes on a mind of its own and just kind of bobs around. "I mean, I obviously know it's okay, but I don't want to be. You know? Like…if I let myself not be okay, then it'll pull me down and the weight of everything that just keeps coming will crush me…As long as I force myself into my positive bubble and handle things step-by-step, I feel like I have some kind of control over the situation." I release a big breath that I'd been holding in while trying to get that all out at once.

She's just nodding again; her gaze feels like she can see everything. "That makes perfect sense. Just promise me, if you need to take the time to not be okay, you'll let someone know so we can be there to help."

"I promise," I say with a large smile on my face, pushing the negatives back down into their hole where they belong.

"Now," Willa begins, leaning back into her own seat. "Regarding the prophecy."

I lean forward, hanging on her every word.

"There is a place where all prophecies are kept. We don't know why they began to gather there, but once we discovered it, we were able to keep it protected—"

"Perfect! Where is it?"

She smiles fondly at me. "That's the thing. It's not here."

"What, like, not near campus? That's fine; I wouldn't expect it to be."

She releases a light chuckle, shaking her head. "No, Leera, it's not in the human realm. It's in Sabbax. And the only ones with access are the royal family and the Keeper."

"Oh, snot. Why did I think this would be simple?" I ask, locking my hands together with my elbows on the table, leaning my face against my hands. "What can I do?" I ask quietly, losing steam.

She looks over my head, almost like she's investigating the decorations or the single cobweb between the dark-green walls and the off-white ceiling. I allow her a few minutes to think before piping in, "Willa?"

She visibly shakes off the thoughts or visions she was having. "Sorry, I was looking back through my memory surrounding the rules of accessing prophecies. My last understanding was that, because they have been outlawed and should not be obtained, the person whom the prophecy belongs to cannot claim it. A meeting can be requested with the Queen, and you may explain the situation to her. She will then decide whether or not to grant you access and knowledge to the prophecy's information." She taps her chin in thought. "I believe she has allowed it a couple of times when there was a great threat," she finishes, her eyes coming back to now and not the memories in her mind.

I nod my head like I'm keeping up. "Okay…so…two things: One, can you send all of that to me in a text or email so I don't get anything wrong when I relay it to Roman and the guys? Two, are you telling me I would have to go to Sabbax? Am I even allowed there?"

Her warm brown features soften, and she raises her pointer finger. "One, yes, I'll just send it straight to Roman. He gave me his number after our last encounter." She smiles and adds her middle finger, now looking like she's throwing up a peace sign. "Two, yes, you would have to go to Sabbax to obtain the prophecy as long as you get approval and are allowed to go. If you all coordinate schedules with me, especially if it's during a break, I would be honored to accompany you…should I use your royal title?"

I shake my head with a smile. "Oh, gosh, no, please…ha! I mean, no, thank you. I'm not ready for all that." I fidget with the ends of my scarf. "The guys said we'll tackle that together when I'm ready…but…I honestly have no idea when that will be."

She nods again. "There's nothing wrong with that; take all the time you need." She reaches across the table, patting my fidgeting hands with hers, and her watch flashes awake at the movement. "Oh, I didn't realize the time; I still have another appointment today. Sorry to run! Text me," she finishes as she scrambles to throw her coat on and bolts out of the coffee shop.

I let myself settle into my seat, and Fran takes the opportunity to make her way in and sit across from me. Not saying anything, of course. Just waiting. And watching. I wrap my arms around my middle, processing everything she's just told me. While processing, I jolt with the realization that at some point in the very near future, I will be journeying to the realm of the witches.

14
ROMAN

We finish watching the game film, and the six of us definitely agree that there was something wrong with the Warriors players. Now, we just have to figure out what happened. My instinct tells me they were under some kind of spell. Our rivalry has always been energetic, but this was the wrong kind of energy. They weren't out there for the puck or the points; they were out for blood.

It makes me think my father and his dark witches got to them somehow. But if so, why hockey? He can't do anything to risk exposing our kind, let alone on national television.

There are too many unknown variables in all of this.

Fran's been texting me updates about Leera's coffee date with Willa every ten minutes on the dot. I pushed it back from my preferred every-five-minute updates, but I knew she'd likely be there for a while.

I'm glad she's slowly getting out of the townhouse more and branching out. Networking. Making friends and learning to count on people instead of doing everything on her own.

We've been so wrapped up in all the dangers, school, hockey, researching, that we haven't had much new-couple time. Which I am planning to rectify tomorrow.

But first, my men have to help me finish getting everything ready. While we do, I'm hoping to reconnect with Eris and find out what's really going on with him.

> Hey Princess – the guys & I will be home late.

> Why don't you text and see if Zoey wants to come over for a girls night?

Little Miracle

Is everything okay??

> Of course.

> I promise.

Pinky promise?

> I just promised...

"Benny! What's a pinky promise?" I holler across the room.

His eyebrows scrunch together, and he raises his shoulder like he also has no fucking clue.

> What is this pinky promise?

Little Miracle

The most sacred of promises.

If you break it, you don't only break my trust.

She's very serious about this pinky promise.

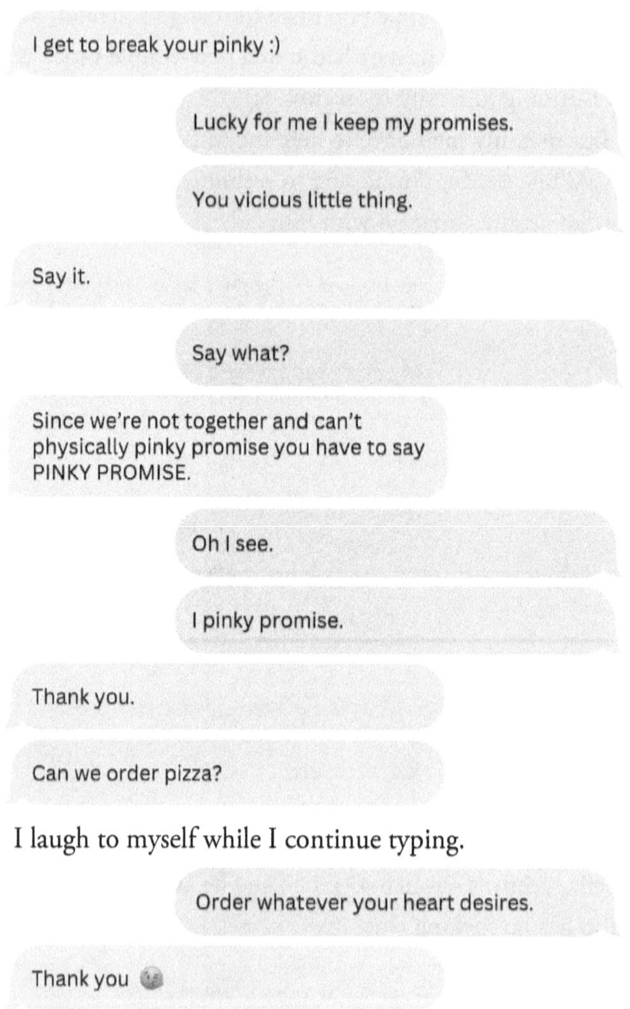

I laugh to myself while I continue typing.

I lift my head from my phone with what has to be the most obnoxious smile on my face. She never ceases to amaze me with her light.

"All right, Boss, what's the plan?" Benny asks, leaning against the wall with his arms crossed over his chest.

"Time to go," I announce as I grab my bag and head towards the exit. "We've got some work to do on the pack lands."

With the pack being further north and closer to the Canadian border and Great Lakes, the snow has already begun to fall, mostly in small dustings, but it's cold enough that if more fell, it would stick and stay for a little while.

With the help of the Pinterest and my powers of observation when it comes to my little mate, I've got an epic date planned for Leera tomorrow if it all works the way it's supposed to. I also brought along a little magical insurance from Willa, just in case my plan doesn't quite work the way I have planned.

While my men decide to take their wolf forms to the pack lands, I drive the car with their clothes, my bag, and all of Slate's electronics. When we arrive at the edge of the lands where I park the car, their wolves all approach, shifting as they reach the car to grab their clothes from the back seat.

Once they are all dressed, Slate and I grab our bags to hike out to the west side of the pack lands where it's mostly forest area and a small clearing. We make the trek there in an almost uncomfortable silence, a first for us. The twins are usually goofing off, but everything's been so fucked up since we discovered my sister. *What if things never return to the way they were? What if whatever is eating at Eris becomes too much, and he pushes us all away?* I still don't know what could be so bad that he won't talk to us and is considering rejecting his mate.

I'm pulled from my thoughts when we reach the area that we can work on the project I had Brutus get started for me. I delegate instructions among my men, giving each of us a task to accomplish. The only task I'm worried about is the ice. I'm not sure it's quite cold enough to keep the ice thick and solid enough for what I have planned.

I task Eris with assisting me so that I can try to talk to him, much to Benny's chagrin as he's used to being my right hand.

We settle into a more comfortable silence as we all work. Slate and Dolos blowing out their eardrums with their "noise-canceling" headphones that are turned up so loud I can hear their music all the way over here.

"Look—"

"I just—"

Eris and I begin at the same time.

"Please. Continue," I encourage him calmly.

He keeps his head lowered as we work in tandem between the trees. "There's still so much you don't know," he grunts like he's struggling to get the words out. I think he's finished, but I patiently wait for more information. "About our parents. The shit we've seen. Fuck. The shit we've done…" he trails off again but doesn't return to the discussion this time.

We've nearly finished our first task when I finally ask the question bothering me the most, "What does any of it, really, *anything,* have to do with not accepting your fucking mate, Eris?"

He jerks like my words were a physical blow before his haunted eyes find mine. "Because she deserves so much fucking more than me and what I can give her…I don't know if I have anything left to offer her."

The pain in his voice…in his eyes is so full of anger that I can practically feel the tension that is rising within him. He really believes that whatever haunts him makes him unworthy of his own fucking mate. "You know that's not how that works. Look at the fucking shit I've been through. Look at the fucking shit I've done. Look at the shit my father has done and is still doing!" The last sentence ends on a shout as my emotions get the better of me. "Do you think Leera deserves what I've been through? Do you think Leera deserves anything my father's done? Does Leera deserve any-fucking-thing she's been through?"

He doesn't look at me; he keeps his eyes tied to the ground, just barely shaking his head.

"Your mate, my sister, was literally made for you by the Moon Goddess herself. Who the fuck do you think you are to question or deny that?" I throw over my shoulder as I stomp away from him.

The only men that are undeserving of their mates are the men like many of our fathers. Mine being a prime example of a wolf who didn't deserve his mate. Khaos' father as well. The problem with Benny's father was that when he was sober, he was the father and mate a man should be, but he had a problem with addictions, and they made him a monster. The twins never told us much about their upbringing. Now that I think about it, neither did Slate. Then you have Andrei. A man with a literal king and queen as parents who have hearts of gold, but wasn't even able to be raised by them.

The worlds are fucked. Not just the human realm. Werewolves, witches, vampires, you name it. There are good and bad in all species of creatures. Some lean further in certain directions, but at the end of the day, every creature, walking every realm, has a conscious decision to make.

Eris better make the right decision.

By the time we return home to the townhouse, the sun has long since sunk below the horizon, giving way to the waxing crescent above. I hurry through the door, eager for a look at my girl.

I find all three of them tangled together on the couch beneath a colorful heap of fuzzy blankets. The smile that stretches across my face couldn't be contained even if I wanted it to.

My mate, peacefully sleeping on the left, with her silver hair spread across everything in its reach and her perfect pink lips parted. When she moved in, I learned she's a mouth breather, and I've found it adorable ever since. My sister, sleeping in the middle with a small smile on her own face, her dark hair intricately braided against her head with a part in the middle, allowing her hair to separate and flow over each of her shoulders. Her fingers are laced together and resting on her stomach as though she fell asleep in thought. A small chuckle escapes me at the sight of Zoey on the right side of the group. Her dark hair is haphazardly strewn everywhere, and it looks like she might even be tangled in it. She has one arm up over the top of her head and the other arm lying across Runa, and her blanket has fallen to the floor. When I grab it to pull it back up and over her, it shifts Leera's blanket, revealing that the arm that Zoey has draped across Runa was done to link her fingers with Leera's.

My heart swells at the sight, and I once again send thanks to the Goddess. Not only for Leera and my sister, but for Zoey. That the girls have each other. Even when they leave a snack disaster on the table that looks like you sent a bunch of five-year-olds to the store with too much money.

I quietly clean it all up, knowing that if I don't, Matilda will, and that woman does too much as it is.

Dolos stops by to take in the scene and smiles warmly at the girls, lingering on the one in the middle the longest. I can't imagine what he's going through, not being able to claim his mate until his brother gets his shit together. He blows her a kiss even though she's asleep and makes his way to the kitchen when I hear an "ah-ha" come from him.

Andrei and Benny also stop and smile at the girls before helping me grab some of the snacks. Benny grabs a few bites of some of the popcorn as we carry it all into the kitchen. My men and I finish off the snacks; Leera must have known we would. I don't know why else she would have ordered eight pizzas, which must have been Dolos' realization when he beat us to the kitchen.

"Don't let me forget to thank her in the morning for thinking of us," Andrei requests, clapping me on the shoulder on his way out of the room, and I nod.

Eris slowly walks through the space, not going to stand in front of the girls like Dolos or I had, but he does slow, his gaze catching on his mate. His fists are clenched so hard at his sides that his knuckles are turning white. Just when I think he might allow himself this happiness, he mutters to himself and stomps off. I want to get mad and fight him on this, but that won't do any good. He needs to make a real decision, and he needs to do it on his own. No matter how minuscule it was, that was progress.

The sounds of coffee sputtering reach me through my sleep before anything else, though it's immediately followed by the smell of nature's mojo juice. Waking to the smell of coffee again no longer brings tears to my eyes, just warmth to my heart when I remember my sweet parents. No matter who gave birth to me, they raised me and loved me like their own, and now my lifelong memories of them are being carried on through my relationship with Roman.

My heart isn't the only thing that's warm, though; I can feel the sun beating down on me through the floor-to-ceiling windows of the townhouse. Reminding me that we all fell asleep on the couch to see if we could stay awake until the guys got home.

I slowly, and only slightly, open one eye to take in our sleeping arrangement and immediately close it again and bring my hands to my mouth to hold in the giggle that so badly wants to be released. From what I can see, we're a wild, static mess of hair and fuzzy blankets. Zoey is quietly snoring with her head tipped back and mouth wide open. Runa is obnoxiously gorgeous and peaceful-looking as she sleeps. Her dark lashes resting gently on her high cheekbones and twitching faintly with what I hope is a happy dream.

Just as I decide to go ahead and fully open my eyes for the day, I'm greeted with the sight that I do my absolute best to commit to memory for always. Roman rounds the couch, coming towards me holding a pink steaming mug of coffee. He's shirtless, his hair damp from his usual morning shower. His maroon sweatpants are hanging low on his hips, leaving all his completely drool-worthy muscles on display. He notices I'm awake, and the smile that stretches across his unnaturally handsome face could make nuns reconsider their life choices. Speaking of nuns, well, kind of, with the sun shining on us through the windows, he's illuminated and looks like an answered prayer with the rays beaming around him. He looks like he's glowing.

When my eyes make it back to his, his smile has morphed from the previous sweetness to all cocky orneriness, causing me to release the previously contained giggle.

"Good morning, Princess," he greets me, and even his words wrap around me like a warm embrace. He hands me the mug of my life force, and I accept it with one hand, using my other to grab him by the leg of his pants to tug him towards me as I lean over the mug between us for a morning kiss.

"Hmm, good morning, handsome," I purr a little more than intended and hope I'm not blushing.

When he's righted himself to his full height, he leans back in with his whole body, and I look at him curiously with an eyebrow raised, wondering what his next move is. He grabs me just under my ass, sparking a fire in my core that can't be tended to with company. Once he's lifted me and carefully extracted part of my blanket from Runa's clutches, he slips beneath me and settles me on his lap, tucking my blanket back around me to keep me warm.

I nuzzle into him beneath his chin, resting my head on his chest and listening to his heart. The amazingly caring organ he keeps tucked away just for me. I sigh in total bliss and continue to sip on my coffee while we sit in the most comfortable silence. We're just soaking each other in while his hand lazily trails up and down my legs and back, and I continue to listen to the beat of his heart.

When I've finished my coffee, I move to set the mug on the table, but Roman quickly pulls me back into his embrace while taking the mug out of my hand and setting it down for me simultaneously. Both arms are now wrapping me in my safe space, and I thread my fingers through his where they meet around my legs. "I love this," I lean into him and whisper, not wanting to break the magic of the moment.

"Hmm," he growls, "I love you." And now he's the one nuzzling into me.

I reach up and take his face in my hands, spending a moment looking into each of his gorgeous eyes. One blue. One green. "I wish there was a word that could even measure what you mean to me," I breathe. I move my arms, wrapping them around his neck, and kiss him, trying my hardest to pour all those emotions into our connection. He answers my every movement flawlessly. I moved again, untangling blankets from my legs and moving myself to straddle my mate.

A small cough sounds from the other end of the couch, and I freeze completely. "I mean, I can't blame you or anything," Zoey laughs. "I just wanted to make sure you remembered I was here so that I didn't have to witness something I shouldn't have."

We all burst into laughter, startling Runa awake, and I launch myself off of Roman's lap so we don't give his sister the ick.

Benny must have heard us laughing and takes that as his cue to join us. "Ugh, I'm so glad you're all awake," he whines dramatically. "*Someone,*" he stresses and playfully glares at Roman, "wouldn't let anyone near this part of the house until you lovely ladies woke up."

I try to scold him, I really do, but I just laugh and smile because I'm not surprised at all. It makes Zoey laugh all over again, and Runa rolls her eyes as all the men filter into the kitchen. "You wouldn't even let them in the kitchen?" I point at them while glaring lovingly at my mate.

He doesn't even react for a minute, and then he raises his hand to his ear dramatically and just looks at me. All you can hear is drawers opening and closing, cabinets being shut a little too forcefully, someone rummaging through the refrigerator, a blender firing to life, and the water running.

I blush and snicker, "Oh, okay." I glance over at Benny, who looks like he just got caught in a game of hide-and-seek. "Well, if that's what you guys' sound like in the morning, I can't say I blame him for the kitchen bit." I hadn't realized how loud they are because they're all usually up and about before I've even woken up for the day.

Benny's smile returns, and he makes his way to join everyone else in the kitchen for his own morning routine.

"Welp, I really should run." Zoey stretches her arms above her head and arches her back. "I've got class in a couple hours, and it's going to take me nearly that long to brush my hair at this point." She eyes a specifically gnarly-looking rat's nest in her hair, sighing in dread.

I pick my discarded blanket from the floor and toss it back on the couch and move to where Zoey clearly isn't actually ready to get up for the day but doesn't have much of a choice. "All right, let's get you up before you change your mind and skip class," I tease. Grabbing her hands and pulling her up and off the couch despite her groaning protests.

"Yes, Mother," she says mockingly before sticking her tongue out at me and trudging towards the kitchen. "But first, coffee."

16
ROMAN

Leera and I walk Zoey to the door after a borderline raucous morning full of laughter and chatter.

Runa had risen from the couch once the rest of us had made it to the kitchen. I'm fairly certain she had intended to sneak away to her own room, but Leera wasn't having it. She had hollered at her, asking how she liked her coffee. I'm also pretty sure, had Runa attempted to decline, Leera would have physically dragged her into the kitchen with the rest of us.

I was sitting on the barstool with a smile plastered to my face—one that I was finding harder and harder to get rid of when a thought plowed into me like a locomotive.

The number of people in my kitchen continues to grow.

It had always just been me, my men, and Matilda within these once-quiet walls. The light and happiness that Leera brought continues to amaze me as I watched her twirl—yes, twirl—around the kitchen with Zoey, their heads thrown back in laughter after they finally finished dismantling the disaster that was Zoey's hair.

Runa was smiling at them over the rim of her own steaming coffee mug. Dolos was watching Runa with a similar smile, and Eris' eyes were alternating between the two of them with a pained pining I still didn't understand. Benny couldn't hold himself back any longer and joined the girls, dramatically prancing and, again, literally twirling around the room.

A booming laugh escaped me from my perch on the island with Slate to my right, and even he cracked a smile. We were going over the information Willa had sent me about needing to visit Sabbax in order to obtain my father's prophecy. Andrei had been on my left before Leera pouted for him to join their silliness, and like most of us, he couldn't tell her no.

When Matilda entered the room, her weathered face broke into a beaming smile of her own, and she took Andrei's seat, not saying a word, just patting my arm lovingly while she took it all in.

It was then that Zoey's phone went off, and she and Leera stuck their lips out at the same time. "Okay, I really have to go now, or I'll be late for class."

Leera hugs her best friend fiercely. "We need to do this more. Promise me," she demands.

Zoey exaggerates drawing an X on her chest and promises, "Cross my heart," before turning to leave.

My sweet mate deflates slightly at the loss of her friend's presence. This is the perfect time to tell her, "I have a surprise planned for you today," I whisper into her neck, wrapping my arm around her waist, pulling her to me, and turning her from the door.

Her bright eyes meet mine, sparkling with excitement. "A surprise?" she squeaks.

"Yes, my little miracle, a surprise. But only if you think you're up to it," I tease, knowing full well that she's up to it and that I would still find a way to surprise her and make tonight magical for her.

She shoves at my chest playfully and snorts at me. "I love surprises, and I'm up for whatever it is you have planned," she finishes, crossing her arms over her chest and striking a bratty pose. She still doesn't understand that shoving her perfect little tits in the air and cocking her hip out like that actually makes me hard, causing me to no longer take anything she says seriously. Adjusting myself to delay those extra-curricular activities until later, I smile down at her and growl, "I'll never be able to take you to your surprises if we never make it out of our bedroom, Princess."

She blushes furiously when my words register in that pretty head of hers.

"Now, go get ready. I've restocked all your girly shit that you like in the bathroom and got you an outfit to wear; it's laid out on the bed." I lead her towards our room with my hand on her lower back.

When she starts to inquire further, her mouth dropping open to speak, I interject, "And that's all you're getting out of me." I give her a final little shove into our room, not following her in, though. I was serious. If I go in there with her, all my planning will be shot to hell, and we'll never leave that room.

Roughly an hour and a half later, she emerges from the hall, and my breath catches in my chest. She's always so fucking beautiful, but I can tell she put in extra effort today. I heard her running a bath for the candles and vanilla bean bubble bath I left out. The combination of the vanilla melts heavenly with her natural honeysuckle and spun sugar scent—to the point my mouth nearly waters when she enters my space.

"You look fucking breathtaking," I breathe, and she blushes all over with a small giggle.

"Well, you see…" She runs her fingers up the front of my shirt, making sure to skim the muscles underneath, "I have this pretty amazing guy in my life," she looks me in the eye, "and he spoils me with the best girly shit," she laughs, unable to say that one with a straight face, "and he got me this super comfy, adorable outfit," she finishes, reaching around my neck and tugging lightly, which is Leera for, *Pick me up, Big Guy.*

I cup my hands on her perfect little ass, lifting her off the ground and against my body, and she links her arms completely around my neck. "Thank you, Roman," she finishes with a slow and sweet kiss that'll make me have to adjust myself…again.

I gently set her back on her feet and take her in again as she rearranges her clothing so they're lying just right. Thankfully, the temperature dropped again with a cold front, making my plans even more perfect if we get a few snow flurries later.

She's wearing a white long-sleeve shirt under a fluffy pink vest that you can barely see under the pink, white, and silver plaid blanket scarf wrapped around her neck. Her legs are covered in black, fleece-lined leggings with fuzzy pink leg warmers scrunched from her white tennis shoes to just below her calves. The colors all complement her hair and complexion perfectly. *I have to re-*

member to thank Zoey for helping me get it all right.

Her silver hair looks like it's sparkling…wait, it is sparkling; it looks like she sprayed some kind of glitter in it after she curled it, pulling the top half to the back of her head where a large pink bow is settled. All of it combined with her makeup makes her look every bit the princess she is.

"We gonna do something, Big Guy, or are we just going to stand here and gawk at each other all day?" she taunts, her eyes traveling down my body again. "Not that I'm complaining." I hold my hand out to her. She accepts it without an ounce of hesitation, and I pull her into me. "We are definitely going to do what I have planned for us. It took too much work not to." I laugh at the adorable, puzzled look on her face. "First, I packed a picnic of sorts. It's mostly snacks and finger sandwiches, but we have about a three-hour drive ahead of us, so I thought it would be nice to snack the whole way there."

She claps her hands in excitement, rolling onto her toes. "This already sounds perfect!" she squeals in delight.

Taking her hand and leading her towards the door, I grab the picnic basket and thermoses Matilda and I prepared, as well as my coat. Everything else we need is already in the trunk of the SUV or already at our destination.

When we approach the vehicle, I release Leera's hand to open her door and help hoist her into her seat. She playfully swats at me, complaining that she can do it herself, but I can't help myself. Smiling at her antics, I place the basket in the space just behind the center console so that she can reach the basket and have all the snacks she likes.

Rounding the vehicle, I reach my door, lean in to set the thermoses in the cup holders, lift myself into my seat, and start the motor. I turn on Leera's seat warmers to take off the chill and let her pick the music we listen to as we settle in for our drive.

Intentionally making a few stops—claiming I needed to use the restroom, needing to put gas in the car, and wanting something cold to drink—I ensure we arrive at the familiar entrance to the pack lands just as the sun begins to sink below the horizon. You'd think I had some kind of control over nature itself with the way the sky is painted in the perfect pinks and purples filling the sunset sky with cotton candy clouds perfect for my sweet little mate.

When I pull into the familiar lot where we left the car last time, she smiles because I'm sure she believes her surprise is just being with the pack, but we won't even be seeing them on this visit.

17
Leera

Ugh, this stubborn man. He gets me all excited for a surprise. Then he tells me it's going to take about three hours to get here, but after multiple stops, it was much closer to four hours. Now I'm stuck in the car until he's finished loading things into the tiny bed of the side-by-side.

He finally makes his way back to my door, popping it open and holding out his hand for me to take, pulling me out of my seat and into his arms, and setting me on my feet, my feet crunching in the light layer of snow.

The SUV's tinted windows were definitely muting the gorgeous sky. It looks like someone used cotton candy to watercolor the clouds, and I've never seen a more beautiful sunset. The trees of the forest, dusted with the fresh glittery snow, all framing the sky, it's…it's like something out of a movie, and I still can't believe this is real life. Ever since I met this man, so much of my life has felt like a fever-dream. The good and bad kind, but today is about the good.

When he's let me have my fill of the view, he pulls my mother's camera from behind his back and hands it to me. "I figured you'd want to snap some shots while we're here. I remember how much you loved it." He smiles down at me, and I always worry that one of the times he makes my heart stop dead in its tracks, it won't be able to restart.

My eyes crinkle with what probably looks like a borderline psychotic smile, but I can't contain how happy I am that he thinks of these things. It tells me that he really sees me. Not just the mate bond. Not the fact that I'm the reincarnation of someone else. He sees Leera. Just Leera.

I choke out a small, "Thank you," and gently accept my mother's camera from his outstretched hand, immediately rushing to capture the perfect colors of the sunset before they continue to darken and fade altogether. When I've taken a bajillion pictures, I secure the strap around my neck, still cradling the camera with one hand. I find Roman leaning against a tree, and it takes serious conscious effort not to drool at the sight of him. He's dangerously handsome every day, but the way he's leaning against that tree right now looks downright sinful.

He has on black shoes that look like a pair of tennis shoes and a pair of hiking boots had a baby. His pants trailing up his thick, muscular legs are tighter than usual denim and almost look to have a gray hue to them, with a few worn areas and small rips struggling to contain his quads. Under his lightly fur-lined gray suede jacket is a tight white Henley t-shirt with the button undone. He styled his hair, gently pushing it out of his face but in that simply stunning kind of tousled way men do. He has one leg on the ground and one on the tree he's leaning on. While he's distracted by whatever he's thinking, I allow myself a moment to capture a few shots of him.

I suddenly want to climb him…like the poor unsuspecting tree he's leaning against. He finally catches me gawking at him, but before he can say anything, I crook my finger at my hunky hockey playing werewolf.

A smile full of mischief and love lights up his entire face. "You beckoned, Your Majesty," he purrs, and my body shouldn't enjoy the way he says that.

When he's within reach, using my free hand, I latch onto his shirt and pull him into me so that I can kiss him. Cutting the kiss short so we don't get swept away, I rest my forehead against his and whisper a breathy, "I love you."

He growls and holds my face in his hands, raising his chin to kiss me on the forehead where it was touching his. "I love you, too."

"Thank you for such a sweet surprise," I sigh as I melt into him, and he laughs so hard it shakes my whole body. "What, pray tell, is so funny about me thanking you?" I huff.

His smile somehow widens even further as he leads me to the side-by-side. "That wasn't even part of your surprise. We're headed there now," he finishes as he lifts me into my seat and fastens my safety belt.

I wrack my brain for what he could possibly have planned but come up blank as he plops into the seat beside mine, foregoing his own safety belt, I notice. He starts the motor, and the rumbling below me does not help the already slowly rising burn in my core.

We've been lightly bouncing through the woods for a few minutes now, and I'm just about to ask him where we're going when I see unnatural lights up ahead. As we get closer, I see twinkle lights, just like the ones from the rooftop, strewn between and around the trees. When he parks the side-by-side, he smiles over at me before dashing out of the vehicle to unbuckle me and show me what he's put together.

As we approach the sight before us, I gasp, and tears immediately fill my eyes. They are…just wow…it's not just some random twinkle lights strung along the trees; he has wrapped trees and spread the lights between them, in two lines, creating a twinkle-light-lit path through the forest. *But wait, there's more, folks.* "R-Roman, what is that?" I ask, staring at the forest floor of the path.

"Ice," he beams at me in the glow of the tiny lights.

"I know it snowed a little, but why is there a trail of ice on the forest floor surrounded by twinkle lights?"

"Well." He kicks at the snow by his feet, looking suddenly unsure of himself. "I thought it would be fun to take you ice skating, but I wanted it to be more magical…like you." He shrugs like it's no big deal, and there's a light blush on his cheeks that I wouldn't be able to see without my wolf's vision upgrade I received.

Another gasp escapes me, ending in a choked sobbing sound as the tears that were welling in my eyes begin to fall. "This is the sweetest thing anyone has ever done for me," I praise him, flinging myself into his arms. "It's perfect," I breathe into his chest as his strong arms hold me in place.

When I've listened to our hearts nearly beating in sync for a few moments, I pull back, wiping away any running makeup below my eyes and laughing up at him. "I'm going to have to stick to waterproof makeup with you, aren't I?"

"Only as long as they're happy tears," he answers all too seriously.

Flipping the cap off the lens and bringing the camera to my

face, I focus the dial and take an ungodly number of pictures of this beautiful surprise. I want to make sure I never forget a single detail. When I lower the camera, Roman takes that as his cue to bring me a brand-new pair of ice skates. They're not the big and bulky ones the hockey players wear. They're the petite and beautiful skates that figure skaters wear. Where those are usually white or black, these are the lightest, softest pink.

This man.

"Will you help me put them on and lace them up? Well, and teach me, I've never ice skated before."

"Of course."

He lowers me onto the log that I'm sure he thought to set here just for this reason, then kneels before me and removes my tennis shoes. He sets my shoes to the side and pulls the first skate onto my foot, lifting the leg warmers out of the way as he tightly laces it. He explained how it's important to lace them all the way to the top, securing them completely as they support your ankles on the thin blades, then repeated the motions on my other foot. He then pulls his skates out of thin air and turns to sit on the log beside me, performing the same steps much quicker as he's obviously used to handling his own skates.

He pops onto his feet and skate-walks our shoes over to the side-by-side adding them to a small pile of stuff in the little bed. *That must have been where he had the skates on the way in. I wonder what else he has back there.* When he returns to me, his hand extends to me, but there's…almost worry…in his features when he asks, "Do you trust me?"

Undoubtedly, I think, but "Yes" is all that I can get out on a breath with him looking at me like that. I lift my hand into his, and he pulls me to my feet. I begin to wobble on the thin blades of the skates, but his arm winds around my waist and steadies me completely.

"Just take your steps nice and slow," he instructs when he begins to lead me the only half-a-dozen steps to the icy forest-floor path.

"Okay, I made it, now what?" I smile up at him, the lights brightening the forest around us.

"When you move on the ice, you don't step the way you do regularly. As you set your foot down on the ice, you'll extend that step, gliding yourself into the next step. Does that make sense?" he asks with a kindness and patience you wouldn't expect from a werewolf in the stories of our childhood.

I nod and try to mentally picture the way the men all move on the ice, but in slower motions. Imagining the instruction he gave me in my mind so I can tell my body to do that and hope that I don't land on my ass. A small giggle escapes. "Okay, Big Guy, I'm ready…Don't let me fall."

"Never," he instantly responds, all serious again as he prepares for me to step on the ice.

Here goes nothing.

18
ROMAN

I move onto the ice backwards with my arms outstretched, ready for her to join me. The tip of her nose is a little red, but there are no other signs that she's even aware of the frosty air surrounding us. She smiles and blushes furiously. Extending her arms towards mine, she takes her first step onto the ice.

My heart soars as she glides into my grasp flawlessly and moves just like I told her to. *She's a natural.*

"I'm beginning to think there's nothing you can't do, Princess," I praise her, pride ringing through my voice. I continue to move backwards in front of her so that I can watch her every move.

She's still watching her feet, unsure of her abilities yet. When she visibly relaxes, having realized she really is doing this, a megawatt smile breaks out across her face, and she repeats the words I was just thinking, "I really am doing this!" she squeals, drowning me in her happiness.

"You must have an exceptional teacher then," I tease her.

Her eyes twinkle. "Oh, yes, I do." She bats her eyelashes at me. "He's so strong and dreamy, ah." She sighs dramatically, and even though I know she's talking about me, my wolf doesn't catch her sarcasm, and his jealousy floods my veins.

Leera's little giggles abruptly stop, and her eyebrows scrunch together. "Hey, what's wrong?" she asks me with concern in her eyes.

I shake my head. "What? Me? I'm great. What do you mean?" There's no way she could have known that easily how my wolf was feeling without our bond being complete.

She ticks her head to the side. "You still looked happy, but it's like I could feel…not happy feelings coming from you…" she tries to explain.

None of this makes sense, but I wonder if it has to do with whatever strange powers she seems to possess. She's mentioned being able to feel feelings a few times now, and I had thought she was referring more to intuition. I shoot off a quick message to Slate through our mind-link to make a note of it and for us to look into it at a later date.

I release a small laugh, knowing it will help ease her nerves. "I promise everything is perfect. My wolf didn't understand your sarcasm and thought you were genuinely referring to another man," I finish with another small chuckle.

Her hand flies to her mouth on a small laugh. "Oh, I'm sorry, I didn't know tha—"

"He's fine, Leera. Just ancient." I laugh when he huffs at me in my head. I take that opportunity to kick my skate out, swerving it in the ice to land me right next to my little mate, making a dramatic show of clutching her hand in mine and kissing her knuckles. I love watching her blush consume her delicate skin.

With her hand in mine, steadying her as we skate through the quiet of the forest with the lights around us, I watch her take in every sight, sound, and feeling. I think I may have gotten some things wrong early in our relationship. I thought that the depths of how we feel, how she feels, have to do with her human upbringing, but I'm also beginning to question that. While I know humans do interpret things differently than most wolves, I don't think there are even many humans who feel things on the same level that she does. Even before her powers began, I could just tell.

Leera feels things differently than anyone I've ever met. She absorbs every moment to the absolute fullest that she can. Every slight detail, every single sound, every feeling she gets from the sights and sounds. As if she can read my mind, she closes her eyes and ever so slightly tips her head back, taking it all in: the sounds of our skates on the ice below us with the creaking sounds of the forest around us, the way the air rushes past her face as she moves through the cool winter air, the feel of my rougher hand holding her perfectly soft one. She's taking it all in, feeling everything all at once.

In that moment, with her glowing like an angel ornament, I vow to fill her senses with all the most wonderful experiences for the rest of our existence. I know her parents left large shoes to be filled with all the adventures they were able to take her on, but I'll make sure she keeps experiencing things that bring her the level of peace she's enveloped in right here, in this moment.

She cracks open her eye closest to me and smiles. "Do you have to stare at me like that? I can feel your eyes watching me."

"Always," I promise.

19

Leera

My wolf is as happy as I am. I can feel her happiness wiggling beneath my skin like a living, breathing thing. Just underneath that overwhelming happiness, buried deep in my heart, is a seed of terror that someday I will wake up and this will all truly have been a dream. Werewolves and lost princesses and secret twin brothers. Don't forget the kidnapping, bad guys, and secret sister. I'm riding a very thin precipice of a double-edged sword.

I shake the thoughts away and enjoy the now. Even if I do wake up someday to find it's all been in my head, what a wild adventure it has been.

I slowly reopen my eyes, and it's all still there. A path of ice winding through the forest, almost glowing a soft silver-blue. Twinkle lights strung as far as the eye can see. It has even started to snow again, and soft flurries are slowly drifting around us. The most amazing man in the world—well, I guess worlds—is looking at me like I hung the moon in the sky all by myself.

Tears full of so much love and emotion well in my eyes. "Roman, this is so amazing. I love you so much," I choke out as I slow him to a stop and turn to face him, reaching for him.

He lowers himself to meet me in a kiss that buries my previously dug-up worries back where they belong. This is real. I've never experienced anything more real in all my life. The way he kisses me reminds me that I'm alive. I can barely remember what life was like without him in it, and it's something I refuse to ever find out again.

He pulls away all too soon. "Let's get you to the end of the path; I have another surprise," he says, like it's no big deal at all. If I were a cartoon character right now, my jaw would be on the ice below us because this is certifiably insane.

"Roman! This is already so much. You know you don't have to do these things for me, right? I'm not going anywhere. Being spoiled isn't why I stay," I emphasize, hoping that's not why he does all the most amazing things. Do I love being treated like a…well, princess, by the man I love with my entire being? Yes. Would I still love him just as much without all of this? Absolutely.

He begins to skate again, pulling my hand and bringing me with him. "I know. You've made that clear. However. If you could see the smile on your face or feel the love that you project when you see the things I do for you, you'd understand why I do it. Seeing you *that* happy brings me a level of happiness I've never experienced in my entire existence."

Well, how the fuck am I supposed to argue with that?

"Okay," I breathe because seriously, what am I supposed to say to that?

He chuckles, and his breath plumes out in front of him in the cold air. I'm glad he gave me the clothes he did because even I'm starting to feel the chill of the quickly approaching winter seeping into my skin.

In a maneuver far more graceful than I could ever manage in skates, Roman swings in front of me, skating backwards again. I immediately know he's up to something judging by the massive smile stretching across his face. "Close your eyes," he whispers, holding out both hands for me to accept as my eyelids follow his instruction without any direction from my brain. *Traitors.* "Keep your feet still and gently bend your knees so I can pull you just a little further." And, again, my body answers his call without any instruction or approval from myself. I just smile and wait.

He starts moving and gently pulls my body across the ice. It's a strange sensation; for your body to be moving without you being involved in the movement. After just a couple minutes of my being lost in thought while he takes us what I assume is the final distance of his ice path, he slows us to another stop. "Don't open your eyes yet," he whispers to me, and I can still hear the giant smile in his voice. I hear crunching as he steps away from me. Then the sound of him fiddling with something. Maybe flipping a switch of some kind. The anticipation is humming through my body so strongly that I'm nearly shaking.

All of a sudden, it's quiet. Very quiet with only the very low crackle of what might be a fire. *Where did Roman go?* I think, but allow myself to focus, using my wolf's stronger senses instead of allowing panic or anxiety to take hold. The first thing I notice is that I do, in fact, smell fire, so I'm proud of identifying the crackle sound. I slightly turn my head to the other side, listening and inhaling through my nose. I still don't hear anything, but the smell of cherries and leather, of my mate, is stronger over here. Willing my heart to calm so I can hear over the sound of it beating in my chest, I hold my breath and listen. I still don't hear him when his warmth reaches my back. "Looking for something?"

he quietly growls into my neck, goosebumps trailing across my skin, desperate for his touch.

"I'm trying to wait patiently and failing miserably." I half-laugh.

Still behind me, he wraps his arms around me and says, "Let's go ahead and take a few steps and get you off the ice for this part."

Once we're settled in to what's apparently the perfect place, he says, "Okay, give me one more minute. I want to see your reaction." He bolts from behind me, taking his warmth with him. After a moment of him crunching in the earth, he says, "Open them," so softly that I almost miss it.

My eyelids lift, and the scene in front of me takes my breath away. I wish I was exaggerating, but I gasped so hard I choked on my spit, and it sent me into a coughing fit. *Real romantic, Leera.*

"Shit," I hear Roman bark as he rushes to me. I have one hand on my knee and one held out in front of me trying to convey that I'm fine, but since we can't communicate telepathically yet, and I can't seem to cough the spittle from my windpipe, he thinks he did something wrong. "Are you okay? It's all right if you don't like it."

I lift my body back up as the coughing finally slows to a stop and look at him with tears streaming down my face now. I'm not sure if they're more from the coughing, the amazing surprise, or my embarrassment, but all three are definitely part of it. "I'm okay," I'm finally able to squeak. "Gasped…spit…wrong pipe," I say in between a few straggling coughs.

He barks a short laugh and tries to disguise it as his own cough, likely feeling the embarrassment growing heavier and heavier around me.

"I…" I begin testing my ability to speak again, "I think I'm okay now."

Roman approaches me until he's standing so close that I have to crane my neck to look him in the eyes. Before he can even ask, I reassure him, "This…" I shake my head, willing my emotions to let me speak, "This is the most beautiful thing I've ever seen. Tell me this was here before. Tell me you didn't do all of this for me."

His smile returns, and he shakes his head. "This is what I was doing yesterday. Me and the guys. I didn't do it all on my own. Are you sure you like it?"

"No, Roman, I don't like it. Are you kidding me? I don't even love it. Like you, there are not adequate words in the English language for me to appropriately convey what this means to me." Tears are now skittering down my face, and I can't be bothered to care. He moves from in front of me to my side, and I fully take it all in again.

The ice path ends near the end of the tree line, and just in front of us is another smaller lake—maybe at this size, it's considered more of a pond. The forest wraps around this magical little space, and there is a small clearing to my right, and on a wooden platform, there is a domed tent that I can see straight into. It looks like a snow globe out here with everything being covered in the snow flurries and the light dusting on the ground. There's a small fire crackling that's settled between two wooden lounge chairs, as well as another small fire going within the dome in a small stove. The twinkle lights extend in a path to both the chairs and the tent, held up by stakes since the trees are now behind us.

My feet carry me to the snow globe, and I take in the interior. Two-thirds of the inside are taken up by a large bed, covered in fluffy white blankets and pillows, adding to the snow globe ambiance. There's a skinny piece of wall behind the bed that I can't tell what it is…a bathroom or something if I had to guess. To the side of the bed is the stove heater and a comfy-looking lounge chair, also a fluffy white.

Everything is absolutely stunning.

"What is all this?" I ask because this all looks fairly permanent and not just for a date.

"I thought we could use our own little getaway space on the pack lands. I mean," he rubs the back of his neck, "I know with you being the princess and all, our future isn't certain as far as where we will be, but I wanted to create a space for us here that was made for you. It doesn't have a finished bathroom yet, but there will be one. I have it rigged up more like an RV right now, so we can still use it, though—"

"Roman." I stop him with my hands on his chest. "It's perfect." I breathe in his scent and pull him to me, kissing him as hard as I can, hoping he knows how much I love this. That no matter where our lives take us, we'll always have this place to just be *us*.

Without breaking our kiss, he lifts me into him and wraps his arms around me, one arm banded beneath my ass and the other tangling in the hair at the bottom of my neck. He slowly starts walking us towards the little haven he made just for us.

He pulls the hand out of my hair to open the door and carries me inside. It's so warm and toasty in here and smells like the fire mixed with the increasing intensity of Roman's scent that's becoming muskier in the small space.

The door is shut behind us, keeping out the cold air. Roman lifts me even higher as his kisses travel across my jaw to my neck. I tip my head back to give him a better vantage point and am able to successfully gasp without choking myself. Staring out the top of what I have decided will forever be known as our snow globe, the moon is shining in the sky, and the snow flurries are dancing and landing on the edge of our enclosure.

Feeling the heat of embarrassment in my cheeks, I ask quietly, "Is there anyone else out here that will see us?"

His eyes meet mine in the fire-and-twinkle light, and I'm once again struck stupid by the beautiful colors. One green eye, one blue. My eyes dance between his, and we both just kind of get lost in each other again. He shakes his head a little, remembering I asked him a question. "No one. The pack didn't really use these lands except for hunting. I let them know to steer clear of this area while we're here." He growls into my skin as he's resumed kissing me everywhere he can reach, which currently isn't much as I'm terribly overdressed.

As if he was able to read my thoughts, he gently sets me on my feet. I wobble at first, forgetting I have the skates on. They might be second nature to him, but I am definitely still getting used to them. I plop backwards onto the chair by the stove to remove them, but as quickly as I land in the chair, Roman hits his knees in front of me and begins to unlace the skates.

I watch his every move as his large hands nimbly work to untie, loosen, and remove each skate gently but quickly. With the skates off, he slides the fluffy pink sock and leg warmer from my right leg. After setting them down next to him, he rolls his fingers into the sole of my foot, causing me to release an unexpected moan. I've had the mediocre foot massages you get when you get a pedicure, but the way his hands are working the tension in my feet from that skate is a completely new experience. His eyes jump to mine at the sound, and I work to shove the embarrassment down again. *You have nothing to be embarrassed about. This man adores you.* And judging by the slowly growing bulge in his pants, he's enjoying this as much as I am.

He gives my left foot the same treatment, and I'm able to stifle the moan by biting my lip.

I thought after the foot massages, I'd be allowed to stand, but I don't even get the opportunity to try because he goes directly from massaging my foot to massaging my calves. The electricity shooting through my body right now from his touch could keep all of these twinkle lights lit for weeks. I can feel the wetness building between my thighs as he continues to work and knead my body in a way I never thought sexual before.

Once he's had his fill of both legs and before he can move onto whatever he had planned next, I ask, "Roman, honey, when are you going to take off your skates?" when I notice they're still on his feet.

"Would you like me to remove them?" he returns my question with one of his own, and the gravel in his voice skitters across my skin, and all I can do is nod.

He quickly moves to do as I've asked and returns to me, offering me his hand, then pulling me to my feet. He leans in, kissing me again and taking all my brain power with him. I'm clutching his shirt, desperate to hold on to anything to ground me as he unwinds my scarf from around my neck and tosses it onto the back of the chair.

With the scarf gone and my brain still malfunctioning under the spell of his kiss, I barely register him unzipping and slowly guiding my arms out of my fluffy vest. The vest plopping onto the floor snaps me out of it, and I'm suddenly tugging on his jacket. He helps me remove his jacket, and I immediately move for his shirt, only being able to lift it so far because he's so tall he helps me and lifts it off over his head. I can't contain myself, and my fingers move to the chiseled muscles in front of me, letting my fingers trace every dip and ridge, soaking my panties even further.

"Your turn," is all the notice I'm given before he's pulling my long-sleeve shirt over my head, my arms now straight up in the air, leaving me in the silver lace bra I got just last weekend.

"No ripping these. They're my new favorite," I mock-scold with my finger pointed at him.

He throws his head back and laughs. "Now where's the fun in that?" He then huffs, "You should know by now to buy multiples when you find a favorite."

Before I can retort, I'm lifted off of my feet and back into his arms. My legs instinctively wrap around his waist, and my mouth crashes against his. This kiss is different. This kiss is raw and filled with need. My arms are wound around his neck, pulling him into me, and it still doesn't feel close enough. I can't get enough.

He turns with me still attached to his torso like a marsupial and lowers me onto my back. The kiss breaks, and my chest is heaving trying to get enough oxygen to chase away the fog of lust, but it's not working. Not like when I went through my first heat, just in a way that won't go away until I get what I want. Everything I want.

He rises to his full height and flips a switch, turning off the main lights within our little snow globe, as well as the twinkle lights following the ice path, leaving us only illuminated by the moon and the small fire to our side.

I wriggle with need on the fluffy blankets, and a whimper escapes me. Roman inhales a deep breath, and when he opens his eyes, they're blown with need themselves.

He leans and runs his finger along the waistband of my leggings, asking for permission to remove them. I nod furiously, another whimper leaving my lips.

His growl reverberates around the room as his eyes drape over my skin, taking all of me in, his eyes lingering over my silver lingerie set. I take the opportunity to lift myself, lean forward, and unbutton his pants while never breaking eye contact. His dick is pressed so tightly against his jeans that it springs free of the denim the moment I pop the button and begin to lower the zipper, though still held by the confines of his black boxer briefs. Without hesitation, I grab the waistband of those as well, pulling them down with his jeans.

His thick length bobs at eye level when I sit back up from helping him step out of his pants, and I lick my lips in anticipation. The tip is red and looks angry from being confined in his too-tight pants, so I lick around the top, taking the silky-smooth staff in my hand. He tosses his head back, groaning in approval. Though he only allows me a moment to lick around his tip and down the bulging vein while my fingers trail lightly up and down, remembering to pay special attention to his knot. I love listening to his body react to my touch. The power in being able to make him feel this way. He reaches down and lifts my chin so that we're looking into each other's eyes. "Lay back for me," he breathes, and I swear I can see his heart trying to beat out of his chest.

It's hard to look sexy when you drop back onto your elbows and shimmy further onto the bed, but I do the best I can. His face gives nothing away to tell me if I look like a fool. He's still looking at me like I'm some kind of treasure he's found after a lifetime of searching.

He moves across the bed to join me, covering my body with his as he kisses me again. Our bodies touching in so many places has my core begging for attention. "Please," I beg as I take ragged breaths and arch my body into his.

"Yes, Princess," he says as he begins kissing his way down my body. "Your wish is my command," he continues between kisses until he's exactly where I want him. "Are you wet and ready for me?" he asks even though he knows damn well I am. He can smell it. Hell, he can probably see it. There's no way I haven't soaked through these panties.

Forgetting my earlier scold, he elongates a single claw and snaps them right off my body, but my words catch in my throat when he begins to massage his finger into my most sensitive spot.

His tongue quickly replaces his finger, and I cry out at the warmth of his touch. He growls as he eats me, and the vibrations on my clit have me already so close to coming. As if he knows, he slides two fingers in, gently massaging and stretching me as his tongue continues the perfect rhythm that has an orgasm shooting through me so quickly I didn't even feel it building. I scream his name and pull him away by his hair, my clit needing a moment without stimulation to come back down.

He makes a show of licking his lips and fingers, not letting a drop of my release go to waste.

Once the high of my orgasm fades, a sigh leaves me. It's amazing, but I want more. I want everything.

"Roman, pl—"

"Shhh, my little miracle, I know," he soothes, and my eyes immediately fill with tears.

"We can—"

"Yes, Leera. Are you sure you're ready? If you thought there was no turning back before, this is your absolute last chance." He tries to play the question off as a joke, but I can see the worry in his eyes, and I can feel it crackling in the air around us like the fire. It breaks my heart that he thinks that there's absolutely anywhere else I'd rather be.

I nod and whimper, "Please, Roman. I need you. All of you. I love you. Make me yours."

His lips crash into mine again, and I can still taste myself on his lips, but I don't care. I need him. I need him inside me, to complete me. I need him to mark me, to claim me. My soul won't feel complete until he does, and I can't stand this nagging feeling of my missing piece.

When he pulls away from the kiss, he rests his forehead on mine. "I'll be as gentle as I can. It will be uncomfortable at first, then it will hurt a little bit. When the pain fades, it will only ever feel amazing. I promise."

My nerves are shooting through every corner of my body, but I'm ready, so I nod again, pulling him against me.

He leans onto his left forearm, laying it on the side of my head. Now he's lifting my chin with his right hand to kiss me again, the softness returning. When he pulls away, our eyes move together to where his length lies between us. He takes the shaft in his hands and begins to move his head through my folds, gathering what remains of my release. The friction alone helps to calm me, the need drowning the nerves. He rubs it higher, making sure to drag it across my clit.

"Please, Roman. I-I'm ready. I need you."

"I need you too, Princess." He moves the head of his length to my entrance, and I suck in a deep breath. "You have to keep breathing, baby," he instructs, so I release the large breath I was holding, and he begins to move inside of me.

"Oh, God," I breathe, throwing my head back against the

bed.

He freezes and searches my face. "Are you okay?"

"Yes, Roman. Please move. Keep going," I pant, needing him to move.

He moves in another inch, and I start to see stars. I'm so full. He's so big. It's such a tight fit. *Come on, Leera. Now is not the time to panic. Breathe.*

He nearly reaches my resistance, and he's pulling back so slowly I swear I'm going to die. "R-Roman," I stutter. His face looks pained. *Can he feel me panicking?* "P-please keep moving. I promise I'm okay," I say, trying to convince myself as much as I am him.

He nods and kisses me on the forehead while he works his hips in and out of me, just those couple of inches, acclimating my body to the foreign feeling of being so full.

Panting, I lock eyes with him once again. "I'm r-ready," I assure him.

He nods and stops moving his length within me but starts rubbing my bundle of nerves with his thumb, resting his forehead on mine. "This is the part that hurts," he whispers, and I nod. "I'll do it as quickly as I can, and I won't move until you tell me to," he explains while he continues to rub my clit and slowly begins moving in short thrusts. My body feels like an explosive device; I can already feel the fire burning at the end of the wick, and it's eating up the line fast, with detonation rapidly approaching.

I nod furiously, doing everything I can to not thrash my head back and forth. "Please, R—"

My words are cut off by the sharp hitch of his hips plunging him all the way inside of me, and holy shit. A small scream tears from my lungs, and tears gather in my eyes. "Shhh, I'm here," he soothes, rubbing his hands on my temples. "I love you. I love you. I love you," he whispers in chants as he kisses all over my face while I squirm and whimper, waiting for the pain to slowly begin to fade. I feel so full. It's like I can't even take a full breath. "Keep breathing, Leera. You're doing so well. I love you." His continued affirmations keep the tears from gathering in my eyes.

He takes my face in his hands, and his thumbs wipe the last tears from my face. "I'm okay," I breathe, nodding my head again. "I'm ready."

"You're sure?" he asks as his face searches mine once more.

"I've never been more sure of anything in my entire life."

He lifts his torso a little further off of mine, raising one hand to snap my poor bra straps from my chest, and leans in, taking one of my nipples in his mouth, effectively stopping me from reminding him that I wanted to keep this bra. At first, he uses the same hand to pinch and twist my pebbled nipple before he moves in and sucks it into his mouth. While he's sucking on my flesh, his tongue flicks against my nipple.

He begins to slowly move within me, and fuck if it doesn't feel like I'm finally complete. It's still a little tender at first, but after a couple of passes, the pain is nearly all gone, and all that's left is a need burning so big and bright, I don't know how I'll survive it. All the sensations being thrown at me are so completely overwhelming, and I am absolutely certain I will never get enough of this. Of him. Of us, in this way. Complete.

The sounds leaving me don't even sound like me anymore, and the ugly embarrassment beast is nowhere to be found. It's just me and my mate, finally becoming one. Every thrust of his hips sends me hurtling further and further into a chasm I've never been through before. The end of his dick hitting a spot within my body that takes my breath in the best possible way.

He finally releases my nipple and moves to give the other the same attention while I chant his name and try to remember to breathe in between cries of pleasure.

He releases my nipple with a pop and lifts himself back up, re-angling his body so that we can watch where we're finally joined. "Look at us, Princess," his voice holding so much love, another tear rolls down my cheek. "Look at how well you take me. You were made for me."

"Yes. Yes. Yes." Watching him disappear inside my body only amps up everything I'm feeling.

His hips find the perfect rhythm as he drives into me, and just when I begin to feel the now familiar tingle of my orgasm gathering at the bottom of my spine, he stops.

"Wh-what's wrong?" I cry.

"Absolutely nothing. I just want to prepare you for the next part."

Oh, right, I forgot there was more. I nod, wriggling in his hold, creating absolutely any friction I can and doing my best not to mewl.

"When you come this time, I'll be following right behind you, and when I do, my knot will be yours and so will my mark," he pants, offering me short thrusts while he explains, "Once I've marked you, it'll be your turn. Just like with shifting, you'll will your wolf to partially shift, focusing on your teeth."

I gulp and nod. "Yes," is all I can say right now. My brain is all fuzzy, and I feel like if he doesn't move, I just might die. On the other hand, I also kind of feel like this orgasm will end me.

He nods and returns to the perfect pace he had previously set, our skin slapping together while he whispers sweet nothings to me. Promising me the world while it feels like my very DNA is being unraveled in this very moment. I'm panting and moaning and thrashing beneath him, chanting and crying his name as the pressure builds to an unbelievable level.

"Oh-oh, God…I'm…Roman…I'm gonna!" I can't even speak as the spiraling waves of euphoria consume me. My brain is being scrambled, and my body is tingling all over with the electric connection of our bond. Roman moves his hand, and when his thumb meets my clit, my body is shattered to smithereens, no longer able to contain the amount of pleasure he's built within me. My screams fill the air around us, and my body arches off the bed beneath him, and it feels like my soul has left my body.

Roman gives me a moment to return to my body, stalling his body from thrusting, but I can see the twitching need in his muscles. When I've regained control of my body, he slides his hands beneath my back, bringing me up to him. I rest my hands on his shoulders and lock eyes with him as he moves his hands under my thighs, holding onto the globes of my ass while he bounces me on his dick. The new angle makes my eyes cross, and the pleasure begins to build again, even quicker than before.

"I'm. Almost. There," he grunts between thrusts. The final jolt ending on a roar as he pulls my body down completely onto his knot. As I'm stretched and filled completely by his length, his knot, and his cum, another soul-defying orgasm rips through my body so hard and fast that I feel like I can't breathe. I thought I was full when he finally entered my body and we became one. I never knew what full was until now. I didn't know what complete was. I do now.

"Leera, baby, are you okay?" He searches my face, his brows again crinkled in worry.

"Yes," I breathe. "Claim me," I beg, turning my head to the side and pulling my hair out of the way, exposing my neck to him. I watch as his canines elongate before he leans into me, licks the crook of my neck, and bites down. Hard. There is the briefest moment of sharp pain flooded by another explosion of intense pleasure that fires me into another orgasm so hard that I can't even hold my head up. My body tries to scream his name with my head hanging backward, but I'm so hoarse from the other orgasms that it comes out as an unnaturally strangled sound.

Roman gently retracts his fangs from my flesh and licks the mark. It takes everything I have to lift my head up to him just in time to see him bearing his neck to me. I concentrate and plead with my wolf to help me shift my fangs…and it works! I run my tongue over the long, sharp incisors that feel bulky and out of place in my human mouth.

Finally, I lean into him, like he did me, and before I can overthink it, I move in and claim my mate. Growling low in my throat as the coppery tang of his blood hits my tongue, and I have no control over my body when I begin to ride his knot, sending him into another release. I moan when I feel him filling me even further, his cock twitching in the confines of my body while he moans my name, his face nestled against my breasts.

Retracting my fangs, I pull away and lick his wound, repeating his motions. Suddenly, we're both roaring, holding onto each other when our bodies detonate one final time, as our bond snaps into place. That's the only way I can explain it. It's like I can feel his love literally washing over my body, but I crash against his chest in exhaustion and elation. I try to open my eyes to tell him how much I love him, but I don't have the strength to hold them open for even a second.

I love you, Roman. So fucking much you'll never understand. This is the best moment of my entire pucking life, is my last thought before my consciousness leaves me.

20
ROMAN

Leera's body falls limp against mine the instant her words reach me through our mind-link, compliments of our now cemented mate bond. The words are also accompanied by a wave of the love she feels for me crashing through our bond and knocking the air from my lungs. I choke on my emotions, emotions I thought I would never feel again. In the quiet of our snow globe—as Leera has named it—I cry, my tears falling as softly as the snow all around us.

Wrapping my arms tighter around her, I hold her body even closer to mine while I thank the Moon Goddess over and over. When the swelling of my knot finally lessens, allowing me to remove myself from Leera's core, she whimpers in her sleep at the loss but doesn't wake up. I gently lay her head on the pillow, and when I rise, I can't help but stand and stare at her. Everything about her is absolute perfection. Her silver hair splayed against the fluffy white pillow. Her eyelashes resting on her still rosy cheeks. Her mouth cracked open just a bit. The steady rise and fall of her chest as she dreams. Her tapered waist that blooms into full hips with small, white, jagged stretch marks across the outside of her thighs. Even her stretch marks seem to sparkle. The thought of her someday having much more prominent stretch marks in the future if she wants to have a family nearly brings me to my knees.

I release a deep sigh and shake those thoughts away for now, making my way to the small unfinished bathroom. I didn't have enough time to get the plumbing completely run, but I was able to set it up with a temporary system like that of an RV until I can finish the project. There are jugs of water to use by the sink. I even remembered to set an electric tea kettle in here so that we could warm water.

Clicking the warmer on, I run my hand through my hair and glance at myself in the mirror. A shocked sound leaves my body when I see the mark the Goddess bestowed on me on behalf of Leera's bite. My jaw hangs slack as I try to take in the large mark overtaking the left side of my neck and shoulder. I move my body to get a better look as the mark begins where she claimed me.

The mark is made up of silver lines ingrained in my golden-tanned flesh. The silver lines are sharp, jagged, and bold, not unlike me. The organization of the lines looks as though it creates some kind of large image, maybe a flower that looks like the sun, or vice versa, and that strange shape is surrounded by the lines moving in all directions, reaching out from the center, in the same sharp movements. It looks like some kind of expensive tattoo a human would get, and I can't stop just staring in awe at my little miracle mate's mark.

The warmer beeps, letting me know the water is an acceptable temperature, drawing my attention back to the task at hand. I give my mark one more run of my gaze, brushing my fingers along some of the line work, then turn to grab a washcloth. Taking the warm water and small towel with me back into the main room, I kneel by Leera's side of the bed and clean her up. She releases a small moan in her sleep, and I have to audibly scold my dick, who thinks that means we get to spend more time inside of her.

When I've got her all cleaned up, I take everything back to the bathroom and clean myself quickly before returning to my princess. I can't see her mark because she's lying on it. We each left our marks on the other's left side, and she's currently lying on hers.

Pulling the covers up and over us both, I allow myself to stare out of the top of the clear ceiling, revealing an obnoxious number of stars. All of them are burning and sparkling, completely unaware that the world will never be the same. My world will never be the same, and neither will a single being that's ever so much as thought of hurting her. It doesn't matter how long it takes, every single one of them will perish…painfully.

Returning my focus to the stunningly perfect creature beside me, I roll onto my side, pulling her into me. Her body is warm and soft against mine, and my continued thanks to the Goddess sound like a chant at this point. With our bodies securely locked together, I tuck the blankets around the front of her so she doesn't knock it loose in her sleep.

I'm jolted awake from a very deep sleep by the screams of my mate, and all my worst nightmares take turns flying through my mind. By the time I've thrown myself out of bed and landed on my feet, I can feel Leera's happiness and love flying down our mate bond so hard that it knocks me back onto my ass, on the edge of the bed. Now that I nearly have my bearings, I can tell the difference in her pitch. She's not screaming. She's squealing. The noise she and Zoey make when they're very excited about something, only majorly personified.

Shaking the fear from my mind with the adrenaline now surging through my veins, I stand and make my way to the small bathroom to find her bouncing on her feet in front of the mirror. If I thought my mark was incredible, hers is…well, fit for my princess.

"Roman! Look at it!" she squeals again when she catches me gawking at her. She turns to fully face me, still naked from last night, and there are tears starting to trickle down her face.

"Hey, hey, hey, what's wrong?" I ask smoothly as I lunge to wrap her in my arms, everywhere our skin touches sending tremors through my muscles.

She hiccups a small sob and lifts her chin to look me in my eyes. "It's so beautiful," she whispers as if she's scared someone will take it from her.

I'm about to speak when her eyes register my very similar mark, and she's crying again and running her fingers over my mark, which is very sensitive, and my dick has never gone from mildly aware to raging hard-on modes so quickly. My reaction must have made it straight through the mate bond because her physical reaction to it is also immediate, so I return the favor, running my fingers across the intricate lines of her mark of our bond.

Where the silver lines of mine are all sharp, jagged, and bold, hers are soft, flowing, and…how do I explain it…almost bubbly. Just like her. It also begins with the same strange base of a sun-like flower made up of swirling lines and branches out into sweeping vines and twirls. If you look closely enough, a few of the small twirls even form tiny heart shapes.

She visibly shivers with the gentle pass of my fingers against her flesh, and it's not from the cold. "They're so perfect," she breathes, reaching her arms up to my neck and pulling for me to lift her into my arms. It's her favorite place to be and mine. The moment she's where she wants to be, she crashes her lips against mine, and before I realize what's happening, her thoughts are tumbling across our bond, and holy fuck, I was not prepared.

Oh my God, he tastes so good…Is it too soon to have sex again… Fuck, I love him…

I try to remove myself from her lips so I can tell her, but she tightens her hold on my neck, refusing to pull away from me. She begins trying to move herself just enough to grant her some friction against my body. I take her cue, and using one arm wrapped under her to hold her in place, the other comes between us, pinching and lightly twisting her nipples first. She moans into my mouth, *Oh, yes, I love when he twists them like that.*

I do as the lady says and twist them a little harder than I had before, and her head falls back a couple of inches to arch into me, and she moans again. "Leera, I should tell you—"

I'm silenced with her finger on my lips. While I tried to tell her, I could tell her through our link, but I think I'll wait until after she's told me exactly everything she needs. I walk her back to the bed where we tumble into the plush bedding together, and I can feel her giggle all the way to my dick. It's a magical sound that I can't wait to hear for the rest of my existence.

Adjusting us so that she's lying on her back and looking up at me with her wide, icy-blue eyes blown with lust, I lean in and kiss her forehead while I trail my fingers against her skin, everywhere I can reach.

Yes, yes, yes, she chants, still wiggling beneath me. I make a path of kisses moving down the side of her neck, closing in on the fresh mate mark consuming her flesh. When my lips reach the swirling silver lines, I alternate between small kisses and nips, and she screams my name, her body shuddering below me.

Oh my God! Did I just have an orgasm just from him touching my mark?!

I don't give her time to recover, moving away from her so that I can settle between her thighs, dragging my hands down her body as I go. I lift each of her soft legs and rest them over my shoulders, her skin connecting with my fresh mark, making it even more challenging to not blow early. Inhaling her sweet scent, I lean in and pass my tongue through her warm, wet, sensitive skin.

Fuck, yes, she purrs in my mind.

After a few more passes, I focus my tongue on her clit, flattening my tongue against it and moving my tongue in a rhythmic motion that has her thighs clenching around me.

More, oh, God...please add a finger while you—"Oh!"

I interrupt her thought with her requesting action, sliding my finger all the way into her, no longer meeting resistance, as I continue the pace I've set on her clit and begin to fuck her faster with my finger.

"Roman, please!" she cries in between moans, her head thrashing on the bed. *Shit. It's too much...I'm gonna...*

Feeding off of knowing exactly how she's feeling, I stop pumping my finger and curl it into the inside of her walls, massaging the flesh there and sucking hard on her bundle of nerves while she screams my name, and her legs lock me in the most amazing vice.

I continue to gently massage her through her orgasm, and

when focus returns to her eyes, she slowly lifts herself off the bed and crawls to where I'm now sitting up, waiting to see what she'll do.

I want to…I hope I can do this right for him.

"Leera—" I try to tell her again, but she shakes her head thinking she knows what I'm going to say, so I go ahead and break the ice, *Leera,* I rumble to her through our bond.

She freezes, her eyes snapping to mine, and when it registers, her jaw drops, and the tears return, *I can hear you,* she sniffles lovingly down our bond, and I can't help the chuckle that escapes me at her sweet voice.

That's what I was trying to tell you.

"Oh…Ohhh," she says out loud this time, her eyes widening further.

"I just wanted you to know, but whatever you do for me will be perfect. Just. Like. You." I emphasize my words with kisses along her mark after pulling her to me, and she melts into my embrace.

21
Leera

As if feeling him through our bond wasn't enough, I can finally communicate with him. No matter where we are—well, as long as it's the same plane of existence—we will be able to communicate with each other.

I allow myself a minute of just being here in this moment, my head laying against his chest, listening to his heart beat while his love pours through our bond. It's the most amazing feeling. Not having to worry about how he's feeling because now I'll know.

The moment ends when his fingers run up my spine, grasping the ends of my hair and gently pulling my head back so that I'm looking up at him with my neck bared. The smile on his face is full of love and something a little more wicked, in a good way, causing me to wriggle in his lap as he hardens beneath me.

The first wave of arousal that passes over my body is mine, and as if in answer to mine, Roman's arousal slams through our bond, absolutely consuming me. An animalistic moan escapes me, and my back arches into him.

He leans into me, one hand plucking at my nipples, while

the other holds me against him, and our lips crash together. I'm so overwhelmed with feeling all of my feelings and all of his feelings at once.

"Oh, God, Roman…" I plead.

"I know, my little miracle. Lift," he growls into my neck, tapping my hips. The vibrations of his voice against my skin send another wave of need through my body, and I follow his instruction, lifting my hips in the air. With myself slightly suspended, he runs the head of his dick through my wet center, then circles my clit.

I'm whimpering with need now, *I need you,* I intentionally purr through the bond, very effectively getting his attention. He freezes, locking eyes with me, and lining himself up for me to sink onto. Our gazes remain connected as I slowly ease myself onto him. I don't make it all the way in initially, needing to rise and sink back down.

"Fuck, Leera, you're so fucking perfect," his praise hits me square in the heart while his hands grip my hips so tightly that I wish they would bruise, but I know it's no use. They'll just heal quickly and fade before the day is over.

I continue working my body up and down his length, my body finding a natural movement that feels amazing. My mate inside me, my clit keeps brushing against him, and one of his hands is still plucking and twisting my nipples.

I would ask him if it feels good, but I can feel his happiness and pleasure just as strongly as mine now. That kind of power, knowing for certain that this man—my mate—craves my body the way I crave his, nearly pushes me off the cliff. My hips and movements become erratic as I moan and chant his name, all the while, he moans and groans and says my name like a prayer.

With my orgasm trying to crest, I feel like…"Roman, I can't!" I scream suddenly, and he takes over without a hitch. Locking my hips in place with both hands, he ruts into me, thrusting his hips up, hitting a completely different place inside me than I was reaching by riding him.

"Yes. Yes. Yes," I cry so close to my release when one hand finds my clit, and he bottoms out, shoving his knot inside me, and I'm absolutely destroyed. Screaming his name and holding onto his shoulders for dear life, trying to stay grounded here with him. With his knot locked inside of me, he roars his release, and I can't hold myself up anymore, melting against his chest, slick with sweat.

He awkwardly scooches us back so that he can lean against the headboard of the small bed, both of us panting. I can feel his knot pulsing, and fuck if it doesn't feel good. *God, I just came. Why does it feel like it's rising again?*

That must have made it to him through the bond because he brings his hands back to give my body what it needs. I'm wriggling on his knot because being stretched like this feels so amazing. He rubs circles on my clit before another wicked smile crosses his handsome face. I'm almost there when he pulls his hand from my clit and pulls me to him. "Roman," I beg without an ounce of embarrassment, for once, but he doesn't say anything.

He pulls my body even tighter against his and starts bucking up into me again. Just as the wave begins to crest, he bites down on my fresh mate mark without his fangs, but my senses leave me when the orgasm rips through my body. My vision goes black, and I can't breathe, I can't scream, I can't even hear. It must only be a second, but it feels like an eternity until I can hear again, and Roman is also finding his second release, still locked inside of me.

"Holy. Shit," I pant against him. I'm happy to melt into a Leera puddle lying on his body until I can extract myself from him, but he's not having it. He takes my face in his hands, bringing his lips to every inch of my face, peppering me with sweet little kisses while he praises me and worries over me.

Are you okay…I love you so much…You're so perfect…Are you sure you're okay? You're absolutely everything… he continues until I feel our mixed releases begin to trickle out of me, meaning his knot has deflated enough that I could probably remove myself, but I'm also not quite ready.

"Will it always be like this?" I whisper, not wanting to break the moment.

His head pops up, eyes searching mine. "Being loved with everything I am? Absolutely," he beams at me.

"I meant the intensity of it all," I laugh at him as his eyes sparkle at me. "I thought it was a lot before, but just now…with our bond…" *Dammit.* I can't keep the tears from returning, and he moves to cradle my body against his.

"Shhhh, it's okay, Princess. I've got you," he soothes.

"I know. It's just so much…I didn't know I could love and be loved like this," I confess.

"Oh, baby, we're just getting started." He smiles, and I decide right there we're just going to stay in the fluffy bed of our little snow globe for the rest of the day.

After a wonderful and totally perfect, nearly-twenty-four hours, it's time to pack our stuff up and head home.

I can't stop smiling, and I'm irritated that it's winter, and I can't just wear off-the-shoulder and sleeveless shirts all the time. I never want to cover my mark. I want the entire world to see it, though most people will just think we got these weirdly beautiful, matching tattoos. But I'm okay with that assumption too.

"How will I explain my mark to Zoey?" I realize out loud, turning to look at Roman as he takes the bags from my hands.

He thinks it over to himself for a moment before he answers me, "I say wait until the right moment. She's your best friend, and I trust her, but don't rush it. Maybe don't show her for a little while, and give yourself time to process everything we have going on before you tackle another obstacle?" he suggests, and I nod, because he's right.

Standing by the side-by-side with my arms crossed across my chest, I stare at the little oasis my mate made for me and allow the time we spent here to wash over me. I know we have to leave and head back to the real world, but I definitely have an attachment to this place. "When can we come back?" I ask longingly, and we haven't even left yet.

Roman laughs, wrapping his arms around me and resting his head on my shoulder. "Well, we have a lot coming up, but as soon as we have even an extra evening, I promise to bring you back."

I nod, turning my head around to plant a soft kiss on his lips, any more than that and I'll really never be able to leave. The time we spent here was a blissful blur of a unity and lust-filled haze. Roman explained to me that it's natural for a newly-mated couple to have intense desires for quite some time. Even not mounting him right here and now is a constant struggle of my willpower. Everything he does, every move he makes, I can smell him, I can feel him…Shaking away the need trying to once again consume me, I pull myself out of his arms. "If you don't quit touching me, I won't be able to leave." I try to laugh, but it comes out all breathy.

His eyes dilate, but he also visibly shakes himself free of the desire consuming us. "As much as I would love to, we really do need to return. We need to get your tonic from the healer at home, and we need to set our plans in motion," he says lightly, pulling me into my seat and fastening my seatbelt.

"What tonic? What plans?"

He smiles, and the world threatens to stop spinning. "A tonic that you'll need to take once a month until you're ready to have pups."

"Oh!" My cheeks flame. "We definitely need that tonic." *Shit.* "I didn't mean it like that. I just. Not ready. Yet. That." My words won't come out in the right order or in a way anyone can understand.

He makes it to his seat, stops, and turns his body to move my head so that I'm facing him, "Leera, breathe. I'm not ready either. I want the danger to be gone. I want to enjoy time with you. There's so much time for us to make those kinds of plans. I'm very happy with just you, even if you never decide to be ready for pups," he finishes with a kiss on the end of my nose, and I can feel his sincerity thrumming through our bond, and it immediately calms me.

I nod and allow my thoughts to run away from me on the drive back to the car, where I try to help him load up our things, but he's too much of a big, strong man to let me help.

Brat, he teases. I can hear the smile in his voice, but I realize he's responding to my thoughts again.

"Shit. Haven't you mentioned someone putting their walls up to block people out? Shouldn't I learn how to do that? OH MY GOD, have the men been able to hear my thoughts?" The worry starts to rise again. The thought of our most intimate moments shared with the entire pack.

"No, sweetheart. I gave everyone a heads up, and they had their mental shields in place until I gave the all clear. But, yes, we'll need to work on that." He just keeps smiling. I wish I could be annoyed with him for smiling at me like that all morning because I know it's at least partially amusing for him, but he's so damn pretty to look at when he's smiling like that.

I must have kept that thought to myself because it definitely would have gotten a rise out of him. It would seem that part of the trick to keeping my thoughts to myself is being genuinely aware of my mental processes. Before, I could just think whatever I wanted, and the only giveaways would be when my face decided to have its own form of subtitles. Now it's a strange kind of awareness. It's too hard to explain, but I think that's the key.

As the car pulls away from the place I'm coming to love so much, I ask, "And the plans?"

He reaches across the car, resting his hand on my thigh while he keeps his attention on the road. "The plan is for us to go to Sabbax. Willa texted me with everything you two talked about and what we would need to do. She also offered to join us on the trip and help us out once we get there."

A smile blooms across my face knowing that she'll be coming with us. The men are more than capable, but it'll be nice to have someone that belongs there on our side. "Don't you guys have a bye-week coming up?"

He nods as he says, "We do. In a few weeks, we'll be off for a week." He rubs my thigh, almost as if he's in thought. "A week should be long enough."

"It wouldn't take longer than that, would it?" I turn towards him in the confines of the car, which moves his hand further up my thigh, threatening to distract me again.

He pulls his hand back enough that it's not all I can think about before he continues, "A week here would be nearly three weeks in Sabbax. Time passes differently in each realm. Similar to your time zones, except the time actually moves differently as well. I've always found it strange that Earth is home to the creatures with the shortest life spans, but time moves faster than so many others."

I'm trying to take in the information he's throwing at me without coffee. "So we'd be gone from here for a week, but it would feel like three weeks in the witch's realm?" He nods in confirmation. "And how different is time in Zabella…for when I'm ready to…you know…"

He squeezes my thigh to pull myself from turning to the overwhelming thoughts in my mind. "Yes, I know. And when you're ready, it passes even a little slower than in Sabbax. A week here is about four in Zabella."

I plop back into my seat in wonder, having another moment where I don't entirely believe this is all real. "Well, I guess any time we want to take a vacation, it's smarter to visit one of the realms and get the most bang for our buck." I have no idea why THAT is the thought that came to mind, but here we are.

His laughter fills the vehicle, and I find myself laughing with him.

"I hadn't thought of it like that, but I suppose you're right. Except for the vampire's realm. Time moves even faster there than it does here. It's why they can move so fucking fast," he snarls, and I can't help myself when a squeak of laughter escapes me. "And why is that so funny?" he turns to ask me, the question brewing even in his beautiful eyes.

"Oh." I cough to try and kill the laughter. "I just…didn't realize you weren't a fan of vampires." I try to leave it at that, but he urges me to continue by again asking why that's funny.

I narrow my eyes at him, waiting to see if it clicks. I can see him searching his thoughts for what I could be referring to, but he must come up blank.

"Lucky for you, I really was always a Team Jacob girl," I tease.

His laughter once again fills the small space we're in, and it's so infectious I join him. I don't know how long we laugh together before spending the rest of the drive home in the most comfortable and loving silence, basking in our mate bond.

22
ROMAN

When we return home, a pink hue has made itself at home on Leera's beautiful skin. Her face, the tips of her ears, and if I could see her neck and cheeks, I'm sure they'd be covered in a similar blush. "You don't have any reason to be embarrassed," I try to calm her.

She won't make eye contact with me, and her voice comes out barely as a whisper when she says, "They're all going to know exactly what we were doing," while she fidgets in her seat.

I've already parked the car, so we're just sitting here together, waiting for her rise of nerves to pass. "Leera, you're not wrong, they will know, but it's not the same as it is with humans. Some packs even host mating ceremonies where it's all done in public for the pack to bear witness to."

Her eyes widen, and her jaw drops open. "Tell me you're joking."

I take her hand in mine. "I'm not joking. Nudity and mating are not taboo topics among any other species I've ever met. I've never understood it with humans. It's part of existence. Love.

Joining. Breeding." I point to the roof of the car, gesturing more towards our home. "The beings upstairs already loved and claimed you as our own. They're not going to be talking about the acts themselves; they're going to be joyous that you're officially part of the pack. You're bonded with us. Not just me. All of us."

She slightly nods to herself, and it looks like she's having an internal conversation that I'm not privy to. I prod on her mental walls she's erected very well without my instruction, "I thought you needed help keeping us out of your thoughts?"

Her cheeks turn from light pink to red. "I-I did, but then I just kind of figured it out," she explains sheepishly.

I nod and finally shut off the car, unfolding myself from the vehicle and moving around to her side. I open her door and crowd her in her seat. "I wish I could be surprised that you've already figured it out." She looks up at me with her large, icy-blue eyes, waiting for me to continue. "Don't shut me out," is all I quietly ask as I lay my forehead against hers.

"I wasn't trying to block you out…I mean…it sounds so much worse when you say it that way." She runs her hands up my abs and chest through my shirt. "I just needed a moment to myself to gather my thoughts and prepare myself. I would never shut you out," she finishes softly.

Grunting my approval, I lift her out of the car and into my arms, kicking the door shut behind us.

"Roman, I can walk," she argues and feebly tries to escape my hold.

"I know."

"Soooo, why won't you let me?" she snaps teasingly.

"Tradition."

She rolls her eyes and laughs while the elevator doors close in front of us. "You're going to have to give me more than that."

It's not often in my existence that I've ever felt…what's the word…insecure…but she brings it out of me. She's a wild card. The rules are different, and I don't always know what they are. In Zabella, as a wolf, everything has always been so black and white with little gray area. I continue to find that while so much that humans say and do is completely asinine, there are some things that they do exceptionally well. Traditions are some of those things. "Isn't it customary for a man to carry his woman across the threshold when they return from consummating their union?"

She gasps, her hands fly to her mouth, and her eyes fill with tears all at once. The elevator beeps, indicating that we've made it to the main floor, but I don't hit the button to open the door just yet.

"Did I do it wrong?" I ask, concerned that I screwed it all up; it was supposed to be part of the surprise.

"Oh, Roman," she says lovingly as she raises her hand to the side of my face. "You're so sweet and thoughtful. It's a bit different, though, the…consummation"—she blushes furiously—"isn't why they do it, it's after a wedding. Do…do werewolves not have weddings?" she asks, and her face falls.

"Not usually. Our mate bond is stronger than any marriage would ever be," I begin as a wave of sadness lurches across our bond and hits me square in the heart. "Leera," I demand, and her eyes meet mine. "Just because it's something werewolves don't usually do doesn't mean it's something I won't give you. Do you want a wedding?" I pour all the love I can through our bond, hoping to wash away the sadness.

She drops her eyes from mine. "No, it's okay. You've already done so much for me."

Moving her body so that it's no longer cradled in my arms, but now with her legs wrapped around my waist instinctively so that she has to face me, I continue, "Do you think I call you my little miracle for shits and giggles?" She tries to drop her chin, so I lift it back up. "This isn't a game, Leera. If you asked me for the stars in the sky, I would hunt down the Gods and Goddesses themselves and demand a way to give you what you wanted. If you want a wedding, it would be my absolute honor to give you the one of your dreams, and I'm sorry for not thinking about it," he finishes and kisses my forehead.

"Okay," she whispers in a way that would make me think she was unsure without our bond that's now brimming with happiness at my declaration.

"One more thing," I say sternly. "All you have to do is tell me what you want, Princess. If I can provide it, it's yours. Okay?"

She nods and wraps her arms around my neck, nuzzling in. "Thank you, Roman." She removes herself from my neck and kisses me with all the same love and happiness I have for her.

We're so lost in the kiss that we don't hear the door open and aren't aware until Benny yells, "They're home!" Effectively startling Leera nearly out of my arms, causing me to growl at him. The embarrassed blush returns with a vengeance, but surprise takes over when she sees everyone lower themselves to the ground to bow to her.

Luna, they announce as one through the bond, followed by dozens of voices of the rest of the pack on our lands.

"You guys," she says, trying to hold back her happy tears without success. "Please get up. I don't want you guys to bow to me," she demands as she pulls Benny to his feet.

The rest also rise with a nod from me. "If she doesn't want

bowing, don't do it."

Andrei looks like he has something to say, so I cut him off, *Allow her this for now. If it's inevitable in her future, let her have this while she can.*

Understanding crosses his face, and he nods before pulling her into a tight embrace. When he pulls back, they lock eyes for a moment, and I know they're having their own conversation.

She crinkles her eyes in happiness as she takes in the room. Matilda chooses that moment to steal Leera's attention with a big hug and whispers something in her ear that has even more love filling the room.

When my eyes meet Runa's, I expect her to move towards my mate first, but she doesn't; she comes right to me, embracing me in a fierce hug that I wasn't expecting, and I choke on my own emotions. "Good job, big brother." She pulls back and meets my eyes. "But if you hurt her, I will gut you."

She's completely serious, so I raise my hands in defense. "On my existence, I will do my best to only bring her happiness," I promise my sister while firmly glaring at Eris with a glance at Dolos. Runa notices and shakes her head before moving away to Leera's side.

Once she's there, the girls are whispering and squealing in that way girls do. I wonder for a moment if Leera has rubbed off on Runa that much already, or if she's just learned how to best communicate with Leera. Being a werewolf-born woman, happy squealing isn't usually our thing, but I will gladly listen to them forever. My wolf whines in disagreement as they hit an impressive octave, causing me to chuckle.

"Let's see it then!" Runa announces impatiently.

Leera looks around in confusion for a moment. "See what?"

"Your mark, dear," Matilda says sweetly.

Blushing happily this time, she looks to me, and I nod, tossing my jacket aside and removing my shirt first, causing a collective gasp around the room at the size of my mark. There'll be no hiding it. The large silver lines seem to almost glow in the lighting of the townhouse.

With everyone's attention drawn to me, Leera removes her jacket and pulls the neck of her shirt over, revealing her intricately woven, delicate match to my mark. Everyone gasps again as they take it in, and I pull her to my side.

Is something wrong with our marks? she asks nervously.

No, Princess, I nuzzle into the top of her head. *They're just very large and uniquely colored compared to most mate bond marks we've seen.*

Why didn't you tell me that? So I could have been prepared.

You mean so you could have had more time to overthink it? I ask honestly, raising an eyebrow, challenging her to tell me I'm wrong.

As I expected, she scoffs and doesn't have anything else to say.

Andrei moves closer, his mouth agape. "Leera?" he asks to get her attention.

She swings around to him and sees the look on his face. "What is it?"

He registers his worry and schools his features, seeming to consider his words, then turns to me. "Roman, do your marks look familiar?"

My eyebrows draw together in confusion. "Should it?"

"It would seem that the advisor and your father kept you even farther out of the loop than I imagined," he begins. "Your marks resemble the royal seal that was to be changed following the birth of the princess. As part of a weeklong celebration to express our gratitude to the Moon Goddess for our birth—though every-one only knew of the princess—the King and Queen planned to change all royal seals, banners, symbols…everything to a symbol of a Moon Flower in mid-bloom," he finishes in awe.

Leera quickly pulls out her phone and types up a quick search for a Moon Flower in mid-bloom. She obviously finds what she's looking for while we all watch intently as her mouth drops open in shock; turning her phone to face me, and on the screen plain-as-day, I see a photo of the blooming stages of a Moon Flower, and right in the middle is a flower that looks too much like our marks to be a coincidence.

"Wh-what does that mean?" she asks, still in shock.

All I can do is smile and shake my head. "I believe it means that, like so much else we have learned about you, you have been blessed by the Moon Goddess, my sweet miracle." Because what else could it be? What else could I say?

Her soul returning to me.

Her healing powers.

Her whatever-happens-with-feelings-and-souls powers.

Our mate marks.

It's all simultaneously a gift from the Goddess but also a message that makes me grow weary. Leera is—or will be—very important to the Goddess at some point in our existence, and all I can do is trust the Goddess and keep Leera safe from whatever lies ahead.

23
Leera

Returning home with Roman feels more and more right every time. Having our family waiting for us when we return. It's everything.

Right after we all "oooo'd and awe'd" over mine and Roman's marks, we covered them up, and Zoey came over to visit and gossip. I learned that she had lost her virginity in high school to the person that was supposed to be her high school sweetheart, but she didn't want to talk about it, so I didn't push. It worries me that her experience wasn't all it was supposed to be. After that, I didn't want to gush about everything that Roman had done for me, but she insisted, and when I'd try to leave out even the smallest detail, she would call me out and demand more.

When I'd finally gotten through telling her everything, I swear there were literal hearts in her eyes. I was swooning all over again and so damn happy for the life I've found with him.

Zoey's been gone a couple of hours now, and I managed to talk all the guys into watching Twilight with me before they have practice this evening. Their grumbles and quiet noises of protests have given me an obnoxious amount of joy. More than that, it's the fact that they were willing to sit down and watch this with me, knowing what they were getting themselves into. Now that we've started, though, we have to watch them all. I have to hold in an evil laugh at the thought.

My thoughts are disturbed by a knock on the door. To date, unexpected knocks on this door have not been a good thing, causing my body to tense in preparation for whatever it could be. Roman leaps off the couch and cuts Miss Tilly off as she approaches the door. He checks the small screen and seems to relax a little but not completely before the door slides open to reveal Khaos.

"Oh, hi, Khaos!" I smile and yell as I pause the movie—because they're not getting out of this just because we have company—and make my way to my kind-of-brother, wrapping my arms around him. I can tell he's still getting used to showing affection because when my arms first latch around him, his body locks up tight before slowly accepting my hug and even returning it.

"Hey, Squirt," he counters with an ornery smirk on his face. When he pulls away, a flash of confusion crosses his features so quickly most people would probably miss it. He looks around the room with his eyes slightly narrowed before his focus returns to me, almost reluctantly.

My nose scrunches up all on its own, and the laugh that escapes him is so rich and full of genuine happiness—he should definitely laugh more—I almost forgot why I made the face. "Why Squirt?"

I guess he can call me that if it makes him smile like that, but shit.

"I thought it was a good little sibling name. Not to mention, you are the smallest werewolf I've ever met," he says it with love, but it also kind of feels like a jab. We don't know why I'm so small.

Roman must feel my mixed emotions through our bond and pipes up in my defense, "We think it has something to do with her being on the wolfsbane for so long," he finishes with a smile to me and love in his eyes.

Thank you.

He nods.

Khaos notices the interaction and does a double-take as he looks us over. "You've completed the mate bond."

Not a question. It's a statement. And for some reason, coming from my brother, my body flushes in embarrassment, and all I can do is gape at Roman, who again picks up my slack.

"We did. She's still getting used to having normal conversations surrounding those topics because of being raised as a human, where that topic is still fairly taboo."

Khaos nods but doesn't drop it, and when he says, "Let's see them then," it takes me a moment to realize what he's asking.

Roman caught the meaning well enough as he removes his whole ass shirt just to show Khaos his mark. *You just gotta whip those muscles out any chance you get, huh?* I tease.

He smiles and flexes a bit, showing off for me, and I giggle. Khaos just shakes his head and takes in the mark.

"Silver?" he asks no one in particular, and we both nod as I pull my shirt off my shoulder to reveal a softer version of Roman's mark on my own neck and shoulder.

"It would seem there are congratulations in order," he begins, but when I go to thank him, he's not done talking, "I also have some news I think will be well-received, well…mostly anyways," he finishes with another smirk.

I wrack my brain for all the things he could possibly be about to tell us. I am no way prepared for what he says next, though.

To be continued...
just kidding keep reading!

Don't look at me like that.
I love you! :D

24
ROMAN

"**I**'ve put in a notice of retirement to the NHL, and…I would like to join your pack," Khaos announces directly to me, then smiles at Leera.

I immediately throw up my walls to my men, always leaving Leera access to reach me. A couple of them hop off the couch, looking at him like a madman. I honestly thought I'd heard him incorrectly and was waiting for the "gotcha" moment.

"Why?" is all I can get out, but Leera is there with all of her questions spilling out without her control.

"Are you okay? This isn't because of me, is it? I thought you loved hockey? But you're an Alpha, don't you need your own pack?" she rambles as all of her thoughts pour straight from her mind to her mouth.

He laughs again, and it's still a strange sound when it comes from him. It's almost like Leera knows how long he went without laughing because every time he does it, her eyes twinkle a little, and if he weren't her brother, I would probably have to kill him.

"Yes, I'm okay. Nothing is *because* of you, but you may have influenced that decision. I do love hockey, but I haven't gotten true joy from it, just from using it to take out my frustrations on others. While I was the Alpha of my pack, Alpha energies can exist at any level in any wolf. Some choose to never act on their energies and never lead their own packs. I guess you could say it's kind of like a power some wolves are given. It's up to them to use it. With my pack being gone—with the exception of Runa—I figured I might as well be where my family is."

Leera is gaping at him, slowly closing her mouth as his words process, until she's nodding. Then she stops, and her gaze swings between Khaos and me. I realize she's waiting for my response. I haven't said anything. It seems as though everyone in the room is hanging by a thread, waiting for my answer.

Just for fun at this point, I make a show of sternly thinking about it. The moment I realized Leera's soul still had an attachment to him, I knew I had no choice but to let the past go and start anew. It's also logical that he be part of the pack since Runa will be when Eris gets his shit together. He would also be able to communicate with Leera. I can't argue with anything that makes her happy and protects her at the same time.

There's a fiery warning in her icy-blue eyes when I look over at her, and I can't help the laugh that booms out of me, and the room visibly relaxes. "You all really thought I would reject his request?" I ask in jest, but I can feel it; some of them weren't sure. "I was just giving you a hard time. Of course you can join us. I'll get with the pack and schedule an addition to the next full moon ceremony. When are you planning to announce your retirement?"

He pulls Leera into his side, and with the mate bond so fresh, an unconscious snarl leaves me. Leera's head whips to mine while Khaos just laughs. "It's your mate bond. When it's new, the males are very jealous and protective. He can't help it," he explains for me, and Leera smiles and blushes at me.

I love you, Big Guy, and just like that, my wolf relaxes beneath my skin.

"As soon as they accept it."

Having been focused on Leera, it takes a moment for his words to register. "So, this will be your last season?" I ask to clarify, to which he offers a sharp nod.

I nod to myself in understanding. I've been thinking similarly since Leera came into my life. I also realized that hockey was an outlet, not a passion. I've been good because it was the only thing that could make me *feel.* Even if those feelings were mostly rage and adrenaline. With her in my life, I don't need something to get me by. Even still, it's not something I would decide so quickly, but I also didn't lose my entire pack and play with an entire team that wasn't part of my pack.

"And you're sure that's what you want?" Leera asks quietly, wanting to make sure he's happy with his decision but also hopeful. She clearly wants her brother around more, and I can't blame her.

Just as I think of Runa, she pops around the corner from the hallway. "Oh, hey, Alpha," she greets him with a smile and a nod.

I've noticed that she's a very different woman than Leera in more than the obvious ways. Basically living in hiding her whole life has left its mark, like living like a human left its mark on Leera. She's more withdrawn, not as animated. I've only seen her really let herself go when she's with Leera.

I offer up a silent prayer to the Moon Goddess that Eris gets his head out of his ass and the twins make her happy. She deserves to be happy. She deserves to have a real family. She deserves to stay with us forever. I'll be damned if she isn't able to move from just existing to truly living…like me.

25
Leera

I'm sitting on the roof with the fire going. We're having a randomly warmer than usual day, so I wanted to come outside and enjoy it. Decked out in pink fuzzy everything, from my socks to my blanket, just sipping on a sweet-and-salty iced coffee that Roman brought me before heading into his office to work on monthly pack paperwork. My mind is swimming with everything constantly happening around here, and we need to sit down with the guys—and Runa, of course, I have to remind myself that it's not just guys anymore—and really address everything going on, and I know the perfect way to set it in motion. I lean forward to set my coffee on the full moon coaster on the glass table in front of me, picking up my cell phone.

My Pucking Family

I would like to invoke the right to call a family meeting.

Benny

Very official sounding, Luna. Let's do it.

Dolos

Wait does this mean you just wanted to
invoke the right to call a family meeting?

Or are you also calling a family meeting.

Runa has been added to the chat.

Runa

Um…I accept?

You're family now, you didn't really have
a choice.

Khaos has been added to the chat.

Khaos

Pleasure.

My Pucking Mate

Whatever you wish, Princess.

Yes, Dolos – invoking the right & calling
the meeting.

Dinner Meeting? 6pm?

Khaos

Family meeting. Got it.

What does everyone want to eat?

Andrei

Pizza

Slate

Pizza works - I'll take a thin crust with
pepperoni & jalapenos.

Andrei

Chicken Alfredo with Spinach

Benny

Ewwww Andrei that's not pizza!

Benny

Hawaiian with extra pineapples.

Andrei

Like you have room to talk! Pineapple DOES NOT go on pizza.

Dolos

Cheeseburger with extra pickles.

Eris

Thin crust pepperoni with black olives I guess.

I'm going to get a five cheese pizza but can we also maybe do a pizza swap because now I want to try all of these!

My Pucking Mate

Of course.

You can choose my pizza as well.

Benny

You don't have to suck up anymore you're mated.

Ow! Benny shouts through the pack bond.

Benny unsends his message.

Runa

Uh I guess I'll just take a supreme pizza with stuffed crust.

Khaos

Extra pepperoni with banana peppers &
parmesan.

Roman I'll get you a chicken pizza with
onions & peppers. It tastes like a cheesy
chicken fajita!

Benny

Ok that actually sounds really good.
Definitely pizza swappin!

Okay we'll get the pizza ordered and meet
everyone in the kitchen at 6:00.

Oh and everyone is welcome to bring their
own topics to the family meeting.

Would you like me to send out a tentative
agenda?

Slate

Yes, and if you create it in a drive, you
can give everyone access to add anything
they'd like to discuss.

Perfect. I hadn't thought of that!

We should have a family drive anyways for
all kinds of stuff!

Sure, I can talk to most of them through the pack bond's mind-link thingy, but that would leave out Runa and Khaos. Not to mention, at the end of the day, that stuff will take some getting used to for me. I've always just used my cell phone.

Wrapping my blanket around me tightly as I stand, I tuck my phone into my hand, holding the blanket together, and pick up my coffee with the other and head towards the roof door.

I'm not sure if he heard me scuttling across the roof or if I was thinking out loud through our link again, but I'm not even given a chance to struggle to think of how I'll open the door because Roman comes through it just as I approach it. "You look like you could use a hand," he smiles as he takes me in, looking like a fuzzy pink burrito.

"I could actually, I—" My words are cut off in a squeal when instead of just taking some of my stuff or leading me through the door, he swoops in and scoops me into his arms. His body filling my blanket cocoon with the extra warmth I'd lost being outside.

I nuzzle into him as he carries me down the stairs like I weigh nothing at all before setting me on my feet to shuffle over to the kitchen island. "Thank you." I smile up at him, pulling him down by the front of his shirt so I could give him a quick kiss. "Can you grab my laptop?" I say quickly when I see that familiar spark in his eyes. We don't have time for that right now. That'll just distract me from getting things done.

He smiles and steps away to get my laptop for me, returning quickly. "You want to get set up here or in the living room?"

Looking between the island and the comfy couch, I weigh my options. The living room would be more comfortable, but I'll be able to focus better in the kitchen. "Here is perfect. Thank you."

Shedding my blanket, I set my station up at the kitchen island to get some work done. Roman takes my blanket over and drapes it over the couch before making his way into the kitchen. "Did you get all your work done?" I ask as I grab another coaster—this one with a stained-glass red rose on it—to set my coffee on so that it doesn't dribble condensation all over the white crystal countertops.

He pulls the refrigerator door open—his forearm muscles flexing in a way that shouldn't make me drool like this—ducking his head inside in search of something. "I got enough done," he grunts and emerges with a bottle of sparkling flavored water.

Laughter bubbles out of me when he returns and sits beside me with his strawberry shortcake flavored water. I've been slowly adding some of my favorite things to the grocery list, not wanting to ask for too much, but it seems I'm not the only one who enjoys them.

"What?" he asks in mock offense, his hand dramatically placed over his heart.

"I guess I didn't peg my big, strong werewolf mate for the strawberry-shortcake type."

He raises the eyebrow over his bright green eye as he cracks the seal and takes a long drink from the bottle, his throat moving with the motions causing me to gulp. He finishes with an equally dramatic smack of his lips and an "ahhhh" sound you make when you've taken a long drink to quench your thirst. "We'd never tried a lot of the things that have started showing up around the kitchen. We have you to thank for that, I assume?"

"I guess so." I nod, turning my face to try and hide the blush creeping across my skin.

But like everything else, he notices, pulling my face back to his. "I don't care if you write enough things on the shopping list to fill the entire townhouse, let alone the whole kitchen," he demands in the tone that makes my thighs clench. "When you get done with everything you need to do here," he nods towards my nearly forgotten laptop, "You write down all your favorite snacks and drinks, yeah?"

I smile and nod because he's got my brain on the line of fuzzy, and I need to refocus so I can get everything ready for our family meeting.

"Can you order the pizza while I get to work on the drive

and list everything that I want to discuss with everyone?" I ask with my eyes on the screen and begin typing.

"Of course." With that, he rises from his seat beside me and kisses the top of my head as he wanders away.

I've just wrapped up the finishing touches on the Inaugural Family Meeting Agenda when the door buzzes, followed by the rich aroma of an array of pizzas reaching me. I hurry to shoot the link off to everyone in our family chat and move to clear my things from the large kitchen island for a pizza smorgasbord. Roman reaches the island, setting the pizza tower on the right side.

We've got about fifteen minutes before everyone's supposed to be here, so I use that time to prepare the countertop for a buffet-style setting. Darting around the kitchen, I grab plates, napkins, ranch dressing, water, soda, flavored water, and wine. I arrange the plates and napkins first, followed by the pizza. There's also a box of breadsticks and a box of cheese sticks with two tubs of marinara sauce for dipping, so I move those back to the front of the line nearest the plates and napkins. I grab some spoons for the sauce tubs and some little dip cups that I had also asked Miss Tilly to stock in the kitchen for me. I can't stand when my food touches or sauces move across the plate, touching things before I'm ready to dip them, making them soggy.

When it's all prepared, everyone starts to trickle in.

"Pizza night has never looked so organized before," Benny chuckles from between Roman and me as he wraps his arms around us.

Roman grumbles something to him under his breath that

I can't hear before pulling me around Benny and plastering me against his side.

I smile up at him, holding onto him, feeling the trill of jealousy through our bond.

"I was thinking since the food pretty much took over the island, we could eat in the dining room for once?" I ask, full of hope. We haven't had a formal-style meal where we actually all sit at the table. "Is there enough room for everyone?" I realize I hadn't even thought about that. I think there's only eight seats in there.

"Of course we can. Andrei, come help me put the extra slats in the dining room table," he calls to my twin, and they branch off into the other room.

As we all move to gather our pizza, I expect everyone to gravitate towards the pizza they requested, but most everyone is like me and grabs a slice of each style, with the exceptions of Andrei not taking a slice of Hawaiian and Benny not taking a slice of the Alfredo pizza. I also take one of each slice, not that I'll be able to eat all of this, but I want to try them. Pizza is pizza, and all the different flavors are intriguing. I also grab a breadstick, some marinara, and a can of Mountain Dew on my way to the dining room.

I'm the last one that makes it to the room to find everyone standing, not sure where to sit with the new family mixture we have going on here. Where normally I'd be uncomfortable, it makes me smile because this is a new beginning for all of us.

Roman takes what I assume has always been his seat at the head of the table. I make my way across the room to sit at his right side, which is apparently the wrong answer. He rises from his seat, shoves it backward and out of his way before grabbing my seat, and with me in it, he drags me to his side, but also now at the head of the table—always his equal. *I love you.* I beam at him through our bond.

And I, you.

I wait for everyone else to sit, but no one moves. "What are you waiting for? Sit. Sit," I laugh, but still, no one moves.

"It is customary that when the Luna of a pack arrives, she is tasked with the reorganization of such things, ensuring she feels comfortable and has an active role in all things," Andrei fills me in.

A small laugh leaves me. "Well, why didn't you just say so? How am I supposed to know?"

Roman rubs the back of his neck, looking almost bashful. "I forget some of the older traditions."

Looking around the room at our large family and our table, I say, "Well, first thing is that Miss Tilly is miss—"

"Nonsense, dear, I'm here," she tuts as she shuffles into the room with her plate of pizza, her smile beaming at me.

After setting the table with our family, I think I have it down in a temporary order. Runa is seated to Roman's left with Miss Tilly beside her. Benny is at the other end of the table, as he's Roman's beta, with Dolos to his right and Eris to his left. I separated the twins to keep them out of trouble, and neither of them gets to sit by Runa until they get their shit together. To my right is Andrei, then Khaos, and finally Slate. I felt bad choosing between my brothers, but Khaos offered to sit in the middle; I believe even he can feel the tension radiating from Eris.

It's a temporary order because I would hope to sit Runa between her mates when they've ironed out whatever their issues are. I also hope all of the guys are able to find their mates someday. When that happens, how will things continue to change? What if some of them don't want to live together with all of us anymore?

Roman must have felt my thoughts running away from me—that or my slightly rising panic at the thought of our family group changing—because he rests his large hand on my thigh, squeezing gently and reminding me that he's here. "All right, Princess, how should we proceed?"

"How about food first, then discussion?" I ask the group, and everyone nods or vocalizes their agreements.

We all begin to tear into our pizza, and it's an image I wish I could capture with my camera and hang on the wall: Our First Family Meeting Dinner.

26
ROMAN

We all ate until all the pizza was gone, everyone having gone back for seconds or thirds. Afterwards, Matilda surprised Leera with a batch of some kind of flaky-looking pastry-cookie in the shape of a bow with coarse pink sugar on top. Apparently, Leera had mentioned them being her favorite in passing one day, so naturally, Matilda found a recipe, tweaked it to her standards, and made a werewolf-sized batch.

With Leera happily nibbling on cookies and sipping on a glass of sparkling cider, I offer my men glasses of whiskey before we begin working through Leera's agenda for the meeting. I'm momentarily shocked when my sister scoffs at me and requests a glass of whiskey for herself. I have to remember that not only is she here, but she's not much younger than me. Leera makes me apologize for being inconsiderate, Benny and Dolos snicker, and with everyone ready, we proceed.

Leera pulls out her laptop, opening it to the agenda she's drafted, and turns it so that both she and I can see it clearly.

"Before we begin, does anyone have anything they would

like to ensure that we discuss?" Allowing a moment of silence, I look around the room, giving everyone time to chime in. When no one has anything to add, I move forward.

"First thing on the docket—we've loosely discussed this but not at great lengths, which is what we need to do. During our upcoming bye-week, we will be journeying to Sabbax to find what we can about this prophecy. Leera's professor Willa will be joining us. She's a witch and has agreed to be our liaison of sorts. We will want to avoid disclosing that Leera is the lost princess of Zabella and that Andrei is, in fact, the prince. While that information could be helpful when dealing with their rulers, it's not something we want to risk getting out yet." I pause, allowing myself to look around the room and ensure no one has any thoughts or opinions so far. "With that…Andrei and Benny will be going with us. The rest of you will remain here." The room breaks into a cacophony of complaints from those being left behind. "Slate, I need you here monitoring literally everything. You know you won't be able to do that from Sabbax."

He nods with a scowl.

"Runa, we haven't completed our pack bond, meaning I can't reach you if something were to go awry. I'm sorry, but I can't take that chance with your life. As much as I don't want to leave you here." I level the twins with a look, ensuring they understand that it's them I'd rather not leave her with if I had a choice.

"Speaking of. Eris, to be frank, you not coming because for the first time in our time together…I can't…I can't trust you." The room falls silent aside from Leera's small gasp. He raises his head, and his eyes meet mine. "We've stood side-by-side for so long that I never expected this from you. I don't give a fuck that you've got baggage. We all do. I care that you're hiding something from us that is affecting your ability to be a fully present member of my most trusted men. The way you're treating your mate…" I shake my head, ashamed of my brother in arms. "Even if she wasn't my sister, this is unacceptable. You have until our return from Sabbax to figure your shit out," I finish solemnly.

He's grinding his teeth, but his frustration doesn't feel like anger.

He's drowning in some kind of guilt and shame. Leera informs me through our bond, tilting her head up to me. *But there's still a resilience there. Give him time,* she finishes, resting her hand on mine.

I offer her a nod and continue, "Dolos, for lack of a better explanation, you need to be here to help your brother sort out his shit."

"Understood," Dolos says with a smile and assurance not only for me but for Runa too.

Khaos is doing everything within his control to not shoot daggers at me with his eyes. "And why am I being benched?" he asks.

Releasing a sigh, I say, "I need you here. I need you to take charge and protect them and my pack in my absence. I haven't left this realm in a very long time."

My words hit their mark in his heart when he realizes the level of trust I am placing with him, and the irritation bleeds from his features, scrubbing his hands over his face. "Fuck. Okay. You have my word."

We lock eyes and nod.

"Any more questions regarding our trip to Sabbax?" I ask and give everyone plenty of time to respond.

I'm about to move on when Matilda pipes in, "Well, there

is one thing."

Tilting my head at the small smile on her face, I ask, "What is it?"

"Oh, it's silly really, but would you mind if I make a small list of a few things for you to bring back with you? They have the best herbs, meads, and some medicinal things."

A laugh escapes me as that was not what I had expected her to ask, "Of course. It doesn't have to be a small list. Write down anything you need and want."

Leera is taking notes of the entire conversation as we go and updating the meeting agenda for everyone while alternating between bites of the cookies that Matilda keeps passing towards her with a smile.

"Moving on, this is an easy one. I just wanted to let everyone know that Khaos and Runa have asked to formally join our pack and will do so at the full moon ceremony following our return from Sabbax," I inform the group, nodding to Khaos and smiling at Runa.

Congratulations and excitement fill the room once more, with the exception of Eris, of course. Runa is blushing, and Khaos is just being Khaos by doing everything in his power to look unbothered.

Looking down at Leera when I see the next item on the agenda, a small, crooked smile finds its way to her face, but she nods for me to continue.

"That brings us to the topic of Leera's powers. So far it seems as though she can heal, has a connection to people's feelings, and something we don't understand to do with souls. Did I explain that well?" I ask her.

She nods and speaks to the group with an air of maturity

and grace that is very becoming of my beautiful miracle, "Correct, Roman. To explain things from my side to help you better understand, the healing I had no conscious awareness of. Khaos was hurt, and I was upset. I had no idea that my tears could heal him, but I'm so very grateful that they did." She smiles at her soul-brother, earning her a rare smile from Khaos in return. "The feelings are weird and kind of hard to explain. Sometimes I can sort of see them, like the edge of the horizon on a hot day. Sometimes I can feel them. Not feeling exactly what that person feels but being able to assess what they're feeling." She stops and looks to me as if she's waiting for confirmation.

You're doing incredible, Princess. Keep going, I encourage her.

She takes a breath and sip of her cider before continuing, "The souls situation was also strange and even harder to explain. They didn't want anything from me. They didn't say anything. They just kind of wrapped themselves around me before floating towards the sky. It wasn't just after the prayer song. India had done it first. I don't even know if that's considered a power, but being able to feel their souls was…it was so many things. I should have been frightened, but it was an almost comforting feeling. And their souls…with the way they died, you'd have thought their souls would be angry or tarnished in some way. Humans believe that souls that experience profound trauma can become trapped to haunt the earth, never being able to pass on and truly rest…" she trails off, lost in thought.

"What if that's it?" Andrei's voice breaks Leera from her thoughts.

Her brows scrunch in confusion. "What's it?"

"The power," he says, before elaborating, "What if wolves' spirits are the same way? Maybe you allowed their souls to peacefully return to the Moon Goddess without the agony of what they went through?"

Leera's eyes fill with tears, and there are nods and thoughtful faces around the room.

"Are there not any elders that would know? Maybe someone at the palace—" Benny suggests before I cut him off.

"No."

All eyes fly to meet mine.

"Asking around will spread the word. The royal shift was already felt. If we start asking questions, it will reach our enemies, and that's not currently an option. When it is, we will find out everything we can. We just wanted to make you all fully aware, and if anyone had thoughts, they could be discussed," I end with a stern finality.

After another couple hours of general discussion regarding all that we've been encountering these recent months and fine-tuning our plans moving forward, yawns begin to spread through the room, signaling everyone's need for rest.

As Leera and I bid good evening to our family as they make their way out of the room, the energy between us begins to change, casting the trickle of awareness across my skin. While she says good night to Matilda, I lightly trace my fingers up her arm, leaving a trail of goosebumps behind. When I finally reach the collar of her shirt, I gently run my finger just along the inside of her collar. Her body is stuck between fighting to maintain composure in front of Matilda and melting completely into my touch. The scent of her arousal begins to fill the room, and she's biting her lip to keep from gasping or moaning. Matilda shoots me a knowing scold before bidding us good evening and leaving the dining room.

Leera turns sharply, swatting at my chest, her face violently blushing a crimson red. "Roman! Was that really necessary?" she whisper-screeches at me playfully.

Smirking, I nod and hold my hand out to her, and she instantly accepts. I pull her body into mine, nuzzling her neck and her new mark. "I think I deserve a reward." My voice rumbles against her skin, causing her to shiver and sigh.

"And what exactly are you being rewarded for?" She quirks a dark gray eyebrow at me with an ornery smile.

Leaning forward, I knead my fingers into the supple skin of her perfect little ass, lifting her off of her feet and even tighter against me. Her body perfectly answering mine, wrapping her legs around my waist, her arms winding around my neck. "For not ravaging you in front of everyone. I haven't been able to truly think clearly since I carried you down from the roof. I never knew fuzzy pink burritos were my thing," I tease.

She throws her head back on an abrupt laugh, exposing her neck to me and making me instantly hard against her, not that I wasn't already well on my way. She seems to notice as well because when her head levels and her eyes meet mine once more, her lids are hooded, and the brilliant icy-blue of her eyes is quickly becoming clouded with lust.

"Take me to bed, mate," she says in a demanding voice I was not expecting from her, making me groan and stumble to dart through the door and to our room.

27
Leera

By the time Roman kicks the bedroom door shut, my patience has expired. My fingers find their place, locked in his sandy hair as I crash my mouth against his. I don't know if it's our still-fresh mate bond or the forearm incident from earlier, but I feel crazed with need. Not like my heat, where I felt possessed and completely out of control of my body, though. No, this is a need I have control over, and that control says I want my mate now.

His body answers mine in every way, our bond filled with the love, need, and devotion to each other. I remove my hands from his hair and pull away from our kiss just long enough to rip my shirt off over my head. The second it hits the floor, my lips latch back onto his, our tongues tangling as I reach behind me to unclasp my bra and toss it to the floor with my shirt.

Roman groans into the kiss before taking a moment to also remove his shirt, then kicks off his shoes. I can't get enough. I need more. He lifts me slightly higher, moving his hands beneath me, causing a bit of friction just where I need it but stops, and I realize he was undoing and dropping his pants.

My hands scramble for purchase, running along the muscles in his abs, arms, shoulders, and back, tracing my nails along every ridge and valley in my reach. His hands teasingly glide up my legs, stopping to grip my ass and move higher, latching onto the waistband of my leggings. Using both of his hands, he peels my leggings from around my waist and as far as he can until my thighs spread around him, stopping them from being pulled any farther.

He turns us around so that my back is barely resting against the door as he begins to awaken every nerve ending my body with his touch. His legs are slightly spread in a solid stance to support my body between himself and the door, allowing him to balance me while keeping his hands available.

At first, each hand finds one of my nipples, swirling around the rose-colored flesh before pinching and twisting the tender and puckered buds. My breath is coming in pants as I watch his calloused fingers work me deeper into the spiraling need. When he's finished with my nipples, he kneads my breast for a moment before teasingly grazing his fingers down my torso, making a ring around my belly button, and finally closing in exactly where I want him.

But then he stops, with a wicked smile on his face.

"Roman?" I breathe, wriggling in search of contact.

He makes a show of running his hands on my legs before meeting the apex of my thighs, but instead of touching me, he uses his thumbs to separate my tender folds and just looks at me.

"Rom—"

"Touch yourself," he commands in a husky voice that causes another rush of wetness that I know he can see.

I feel the blush rising. He's still looking directly at my core.

"W-what?" I ask.

His eyes finally rise to meet mine. "You said you never knew how to make yourself feel good. While I will be mostly taking over those duties, I still believe you should be more in tune with yourself." His eyes are burning with the same hunger for me that I feel for him.

"Oh…O-okay," I concede, closing my eyes and resting my head back against the door. I follow the same path Roman's hands made from my nipples to kneading my breast, trailing further south, my breaths coming out in pants and moans. I hesitate when my fingers nearly reach where I wish Roman was touching me. Instead, he's still watching my every move with a burning intensity.

"Be a good girl for me, Princess, and I'll give you my cock, just like you want."

My jaw drops open on a gasp of arousal, and my heart kicks around in my chest, trying to figure out how to beat appropriately again. I nod, biting my lip, and trail my fingers even further. When I reach my clit, I tentatively rub my middle finger around it in circles, my hips wiggling against Roman's hardened length below me.

"Mmm, like this?" I breathe.

He leans forward, nipping along the column of my neck, on the opposite side of my mark, sending tingles of pleasure straight to my core.

"Fucking perfect," he growls into my skin before pulling back to watch me work myself. "Don't stop. If you stop, I stop."

"Stop. What?" I ask between pants, the heat rising in my body. I definitely never knew what I was trying to do before because it didn't feel like this. "Oh, God!" I cry out when he plants himself inside me in a single, unexpected thrust. My finger stops, relishing in the fullness, stretching around him, being completely connected to him. I try to move against him, but he tsks me.

"You stopped," he says as his fingers begin plucking at my nipples, heightening my need for him to move.

It feels like it takes my brain days to sort through the burning lust to figure out what the fuck he's talking about. When my finger returns to rub circles around my clit, Roman's hands return to my ass, slowly bringing me up and down his length.

"Oh…shit…more, Roman!" I beg.

"I'm matching your movements. How fast you play with yourself determines how fast I fuck you." He may sound calm, but his last few words were pushed through gritted teeth, meaning I'm not the only one affected.

Nevertheless, I'll play. I begin rubbing my finger around my swollen bundle of nerves a little faster, relishing in the increased rhythm of his hips. "Yes. Yes. Yes!" I chant. I'm so lost in the pleasure rising within me, my body tingling, now using two fingers to circle my clit at what I've found is a pretty perfect rhythm, but I still need more. "Oh, God…Roman, harder!" And like an answered prayer, he holds onto me tighter and begins to plow into me.

We're a panting, moaning, growling mess, rattling the door to his—our—bedroom, chasing that high that comes from our bodies being locked together. Every nerve ending is firing with the electric energy of our bond. My body begins to wind tighter, and, *fuck,* I will never get used to being able to feel Roman's arousal rise along mine in steady consistency through our bond.

Just as I scream his name, my body detonating, he slams into me once more, shoving his knot into my contracting channel, and I scream a hoarse curse as a second orgasm rips through my body, shredding any piece of sanity I might have had left in that moment. He comes with me, but the pressure continues to grow as his knot expands, and I swear to God this orgasm is never going to end. My vision flickers with black spots and bright white stars, and I think I might have forgotten how to breathe as I slump against his chest.

We stay there for a few labored breaths, leaning against the door with my legs still covered in clothing while we are otherwise completely bare and kind of sweaty before Roman gingerly wraps his arms around my body and walks us over to the bed. With our bodies still locked together, he sits on the bed, jostling his still swollen knot further inside of me, making me moan and dig my claws into him.

Fuck! You can NOT be serious right now, I intend to think to myself, but he must have heard me because I hear him chuckle through our bond as my body begins to climb that mountain again, the friction of our bodies still creating an obnoxiously delicious burning sensation in my spine.

"One more, my little miracle," he says in that voice that could make me wet all on its own.

"Shit, okay. Yes. Please." *Why does sex take away my ability to string together a coherent thought or sentence?*

He carefully rolls us over to the center of the bed where he hovers over me, granting me not only more friction, but his amazing cock is hitting an entirely new piece of me. He's not able to pull out, but he is able to push further in, rocking himself into me while he nips at my nipples. My hands are a frenzied mess of desire, holding him, scratching him, pulling him into me. I was going for a kiss, but he bypassed my lips completely, grunting against my neck before biting and locking himself onto my mate mark.

I don't scream this time, I roar. My body arching so hard off the bed, I worry my bones will break. My wolf is howling as my soul leaves my body. *Fuck, he's still going.* "I can't. I can't." I thrash as I cry. My body is completely wrecked, and I know he must be close to coming again because his hips become erratic.

He pulls himself from my mark, peppering my face with loving kisses as he pants, "Fuck. Fucking perfect. Perfect pussy. Perfect mate. Perfect soul."

"Oh…fuck! Oh, God…Roman…I can't—"

"Yes. You. Can," he grunts between powerful thrusts, and fuck, I might die from orgasms.

I'm sobbing as my body reaches a precipice of pleasure that borders on painful. Pulling him to me by his hair, I copy his movements from before, also biting into his new mark. We again roar together as his entire body locks up and stills against me, his cock twitching inside of me.

All I can manage before I pass out from orgasm-induced-exhaustion is a breathy, "I love you."

28
ROMAN

Waking just before dawn with her perfect little body still connected to mine is my new favorite thing. After our spontaneously fierce love-making last night, we both fell into a deep sleep. I hadn't expected to be so rough with her so soon, but I will not be denying my mate her wants. To wake her, I allow my fingers to skitter across her body, tracing her lush curves and soft skin until her eyes flutter open. She doesn't say anything. She just releases a soft, happy sigh.

Without a word, I nuzzle her before lifting her into my arms once more, carrying her to the bathroom, making sweet, slow love to her in the shower before lathering every inch of her body in sweet vanilla body wash and washing it all away.

Fucking her is amazing, but taking care of her in these little life moments is what I refuse to ever take for granted. We don't say much, her still sleepy, just allowing me to care for her. Words aren't needed here. In this calm place before the chaos that lies ahead of us.

My mind tries to escape to worry about everything we still

have to overcome, but I won't allow it. Instead, I choose to focus on my miracle who wanted to return the favor and scrub my body clean as well.

When all the suds have been rinsed down the drain, I swing the shower door open and grab a soft white towel for Leera first, then grab my own. She moves to step out of the shower onto the tiled floor, but I scoop her into my arms and set her on the bathroom counter. She giggles and tucks her towel into itself under her armpit while I run our toothbrushes under the tap, adding toothpaste and handing it to her.

The quiet and happy routine of this morning is wonderfully domestic and unexpected, and I vow to create more of these moments intentionally.

Today, I convinced Leera to walk into the game with me on my arm. Usually, we get ready together, and then the men and I arrive separately for the game day walk-in in our suits. The whole thing has always felt ridiculous. Why do people care what we wear before a game? The twins used to be the ones who seemed to enjoy it the most, with Benny running a close second.

But today, with Leera on my arm in our almost matching outfits, I find I might actually love this. The couple of cameras awaiting our arrival begin clicking as we cross the cheesy maroon carpet they've started laying out for this. In the middle of our walk, I lean down, scooping Leera into my arms so that I can kiss her for the cameras. I would have tried to lean in and drop one on her if her perfect little cheek wasn't so far down.

After dropping my bag off in the locker room, I have enough

time to walk Leera to her seats where Fran and a surprise are waiting. I managed to snag some seats near the end of the team bench, closest to the net, for this game. The further we walk to her seats, the more excited she gets about the seats, not even knowing there is a surprise waiting for her.

The fans are slowly starting to trickle in, all decked out in their maroon, black, and white Predators gear. The Zamboni is making its last turn on the ice, and the music is blaring through the speakers. The chill of the hockey arena nearly matches the current conditions outside, though the energy in here is incomparable. The excitement of the fans is already palpable in the large space.

When we finally reach the seats I got for Leera, Fran stands and nods curtly, not saying a word, but Leera still tries. "Hey Fran! Are you ready for a good game?" she asks her cheerfully, not having yet noticed the other person. "I feel like I haven't seen you in forever. What have you been—"

Leera's words are cut off by her own squealing when Fran rolled her eyes and gestured around her to the unnoticed individual. The squealing is then joined by jumping and clapping because she's so happy. I knew she'd be excited to spend some time with Willa, but I didn't realize just how happy. "Oh my gosh! It's so good to see you!" she raves, launching herself at the witch for a hug before whipping her head around to face me. "You did this?" she beams.

I pull her up and into me, nodding with a chuckle. "I did this. I thought you'd like to spend some time with her at the game, and if you get bored, you can talk about Sabbax." I kiss her on the cheek and pull away. "I've gotta get ready before Coach comes looking for me."

"Oh, right, of course! Have fun." She waves after me before shouting, "I love you!"

I stop dead in my tracks.

We've told each other we love each other plenty.

We've completed our mate bond.

We're solid.

But she has never been the one to initiate public displays of affection.

I slowly turn to take her in with what must be the goofiest smile on my face. Fans with their phones and the team's cameramen are capturing everything, but I don't give a fuck.

She notices the cameras and phones pointed in our direction and puts the pieces together, realizing what she did. She blushes a furious red and practically hides behind Fran.

If she wants some PDA, she's gonna get it.

I march right back to where she's standing, frozen in place. When I reach her, I lift her again, wrapping her legs around my waist this time, and bring her in for a burning kiss that has her panting when I pull away and rest my forehead against hers for a moment. The moment is broken by whoops and hollers all around us, and she's a blushing mess all over again.

I laugh as I set her back on her feet and hustle to the locker room just in time for Coach to tear me a new one for being late.

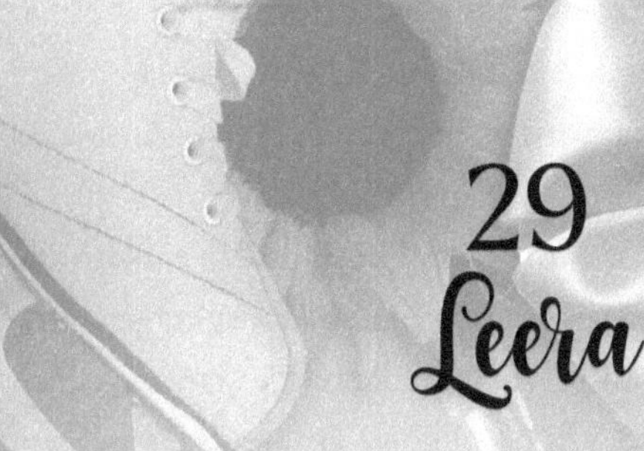

"Do you keep up with hockey?" I ask Willa once we're settled in with our snacks and drinks. The game just started, and already the energy feels off, like it did the last game.

I keep my eyes on Roman and the guys, worried about the level of intensity this match will bring. If I'm right about the energy, it's not going to be fun. Don't get me wrong, I love watching them brawl while they play, don't we all? But this…this is different. It doesn't feel…fuck, what's the word…it doesn't feel natural.

Trying to avoid the uncomfortable and foreboding nagging at the back of my neck, I lean into conversation and snacks with Willa, who now also seems a bit on the distracted side.

We're both quiet for a moment, watching the game with the wind whipping around the arena. It almost feels as though even the fans can feel it this time. All around us is a foggy swelling of apprehension while the air closer to the rink is thick with the unnatural hostility.

"Please tell me you feel any of this," I whisper to Willa, tossing in a nervous giggle in case I need to act like I was joking because I'm just letting my anxiety get the better of me.

Her eyebrows draw together in what I can't decide is either confusion, concentration, or irritation. "Unfortunately, I do." Her dark eyes slowly begin to scan the crowd, Fran also now on high alert.

Releasing a startled scream when Benny is driven into the boards and scares the bajeezus out of me, also managing to startle Willa and Fran. They both jump and take battle stances, which causes us all to break into a fit of laughter among the mayhem. Our laughter is extinguished by gasps all around us.

We'd only stopped watching the game for a moment. I fear the worst, flinging myself around, searching for Roman's eyes until I find them staring directly at me, full of concern. When I finally notice one of the other team's players is laid out on the ice. He's convulsing, and there's a dark gray tint to his veins.

"Dark magic," Willa seethes beside me through gritted teeth.

"What?!" I gasp, "Where? Why? How?" I can't stop my mouth.

Roman. Guys. Willa said it's dark magic.

Be careful! Stay with Fran. Roman fires back, obviously only hearing that there's a dark witch in the building, which means I could be in danger.

I internally roll my eyes while, beside me, Willa begins scanning the stands with more scrutiny while muttering under her breath.

The medics are on the ice trying to calm the player when another one goes down. The gasps erupt around us once more, joined by worried mutterings and a lot of what-the-fuck-is-going-on's. I want to ask Willa if she's getting anything or what we should do to help, but I don't want to interrupt her.

"There!" she yells at Fran, who launches into the aisle and flies up the stairs towards the unseeming blonde woman with her unblinking eyes locked on the rink.

I know it's not what I should be thinking right now, but that woman does not fit my mental image of a dark witch. When I think of a dark witch, I see the bad guys in a Harry Potter movie, or the ugly old witches in the Witches movie, or an old hag that dresses in all black with her fingers tipped in fading black skin. I did not expect to see someone who looks like…well, me. She's dressed similarly and perfectly blends in with the world. Do any paranormal creatures actually give themselves away?

I expect Fran to tackle her in a big dramatic moment, but instead, she steps in front of her, severing her line of sight to the men on the rink, and the men immediately stop convulsing. When the witch rises and acts like she's going to leave, Fran grabs her by the wrist, halting her movements, and looks to Willa, who immediately begins mumbling again, and the dark witch looks to faint.

"Remind me to never piss you off," I try to joke, but Willa's face is serious.

"We only use our powers for good. As long as you aren't doing anything nefarious, I won't have to," she snaps back seriously.

"I know…I just…never mind."

I look out to the ice, and not only are the two previously convulsing men now rising to stand, but their entire team looks around at each other dumbfounded. Was the whole team spelled? Was that the reason for the strange energy and hostility? Was there a dark witch at the last game?

I have too many questions and not enough time to gather answers. The refs call more medics onto the ice to check out the players of the other team, as none of them seem to even know where they are. They can't very well finish a freaking hockey game if they're recovering from some kind of yucky spell they were put under.

But why?

30
ROMAN

The medics call the game and begin clearing out the arena of fans and reporters alike. Fran and Willa left with the dark witch, taking her to the cells below the townhouse for questioning.

After the incident with Leera and the rink's security during the game that I took that nasty hit from Khaos, I got with my co-owner and restricted security to be staffed by shifters or paranormal beings. It's important to me that the people relatively in charge around us are part of our world and don't have to be left in the dark. This situation being a prime fucking example.

With the stands cleared of everyone but Leera and the players who have since changed out of our skates and uniforms, the Crescents head coach and Coach engage in an animated discussion about what the actual fuck happened here. Nodding to Benny, *Stay with Leera,* I make my way to the coaches. "I'm assuming neither of you knows what happened here tonight?"

They both scowl and turn their attention to me.

"I'll take that as a no. All I know, so far, is that a dark witch was here and had your team"—I lock eyes with the Crescents coach—"under some kind of spell."

He jabs his finger in my direction and opens his mouth to say something that would probably piss me off, so I don't offer him the opportunity, speaking over his train of thought.

"Leera's guard and white-witch professor subdued the witch and have taken her to our cells for us to get the answers we need. As soon as I have more information, I'll report back," I finish, looking around the space knowing everyone heard me and offering them the opportunity to speak their concerns.

A satisfied smile spreads across my face, and all the men in the room nod, including the Crescents players, to the irritation of their coach.

Leera tries not to smile, shaking her head at me as I approach her. "What?" I ask dramatically, my arms held wide, awaiting her embrace.

She leans into me, still shaking her head. "You're incorrigible. You know that?"

"I don't care what I am as long as it keeps you smiling like that," I beam at her, running my thumb along her plump bottom lip.

"All right! Time to go," Benny pipes up, snapping the quickly escalating sexual tension. Leera shakes the lustful thoughts from her mind and smiles bashfully.

Back at home, convincing Leera to remain upstairs while we go down to get information from the witch is no simple task. Thankfully, Runa was able to convince her that they needed some girl time before we leave for Sabbax. I'm also fairly certain Leera was very aware that we were teaming up against her to keep her out of harm's way, but she smiled and went along with it.

From the garage, the elevator doesn't go down to protect the privacy and security of what we have only seldom had to keep below the townhouse. There are two doors on the other side of the garage. One is the door to the stairs that lead up to the main level in case of emergency, the electricity is out, or if I just don't feel like taking the elevator up. The other door leads to what looks like a utility closet full of salt, shovels, maintenance fluids, and other boxes of random shit that's collected in there, but if you shut the door completely once inside, there is a hidden panel door in the wall. Pressing on the right side of the door, the digital pin-pad illuminates, and I key in the passcode that only my men and I have knowledge of, and, well, now Fran.

The first flight of stairs takes you down to an area used mostly for storage, though we went through and purged a ton of nonsense out of it during Slate's spring-cleaning meltdown last April. Now it looks more like a weird doomsday bunker with metal shelves lining two walls with some supplies and storage containers.

The second flight of stairs leads to the area where we have a handful of small cells with thick iron bars. Luckily, we haven't had much of a need for them over the years, but they have come in handy on a few occasions. One of those occasions being a time that the twins had managed to piss Benny and Slate off to the point that they'd locked them in here for a weekend.

Standing outside the very first cell are Fran and Willa. Fran's watching the dark witch with her arms crossed over her chest. Willa is scowling, clearly disappointed with the witch.

Dark witches aren't born as such, unless you consider the ones that are raised by dark witches. It's a conscious decision that they make to practice dark magic and to use their powers for evil purposes. Doing so is what divides the white and dark witches, going against their most fundamental edict. It is written into the laws of Sabbax that any witch who chooses to practice dark magic is stripped of any titles or possessions they may hold in Sabbax and are banned from their homeland, never to return.

Choosing to practice dark magic isn't a phase or rebellion. It's not something they can come back from. Once their soul is tainted with the use of dark magic, it can never be mended or forgiven. This results in the dark witches sneaking into other realms. Earth's human realm happens to be the easiest one for them to habituate.

The problem with Sabbax's law is that when they ban these pains-in-my-ass, the rest of us have to deal with them. Instead of kicking them out like a petulant child, they should be doing something about the problem, not handing it off to the next person.

Willa offers us a strained smile as we file into the small space. Benny hot on my heels, Andrei just behind him, Dolos smirking, Eris scowling, and Slate bringing up the rear.

"Anything?" I bark, relishing in the barely perceptible flinch from the bitch in the cell.

The women shake their heads.

"Are you going to answer our questions cooperatively? I really don't have the patience for the whole song and dance," I say, rubbing the muscles between my eyebrows. Being away from Leera makes my entire body coil tighter and strains every nerve ending in my being.

The witch laughs and prepares for what I expect is her well-rehearsed monologue that I don't have the time or energy for. Raising my hand, I interject, "I'm gonna stop you right there. I just wanted to grant you the opportunity to get through this with some of whatever sanity you have left."

I turn to each person standing around me. "Fran, you are dismissed unless you'd like to participate further. Willa, can you make sure she doesn't pull any magic shit on them?"

They both nod.

"Eris, I would have allowed you to take the lead on this, but as you've chosen to keep your head firmly planted up your ass, your services are also not needed."

He mumbles a few curses before stomping back up the stairs without a fight.

"Slate and Dolos, she's all yours. Get us whatever information you are able."

Dolos dramatically cracks his knuckles. "You got it, Boss. Who's ready to party?!" he hollers, echoing in the small space.

Slate rolls his eyes before opening up his laptop and setting it to the side. "We've got it from here," he states firmly.

Turning to head back up the stairs and towards the reason for my existence, I let Benny and Andrei know they can sit in if they'd like, but it's not required. The six of us work like a well-oiled machine—or at least all six of us used to. It's strange not being able to rely on one of the people I've always trusted most.

We haven't had a lot of our old style of action in quite some time, so I imagine Benny is likely chomping at the bit to be involved.

"Don't forget to educate her that if we have to, we'll take her to the prison in Sabbax when we holiday in the far to near future," I toss over my shoulder as I continue to climb the stairs.

31
Leera

The last couple of weeks have been a borderline shit show. Between everything that happened at the game with the players being spelled, Eris' attitude, spending time with Zoey, finishing my classwork for the semester, and preparing myself for this trip, I am both mentally and physically drained. The trip especially.

This isn't just another trip abroad. This trip begins abroad, and then I'll be going to a completely different realm, and not the one I'm a lost-freaking-princess of. I can't seem to wrap my head around the fact that I will be on a completely different plane of existence. Like I'd absorbed the information I'd been given. I've seen werewolves and witches alike. But there's something about going there that I just can't seem to process.

I keep trying to relax, but it's just so much. Roman's taken my wolf out on a few runs with his, and it seems to help. When I let my wolf take over, I can pretend that all the troubles of the real world can't reach me. The wind rushing through my fur. The pads of all four of my paws hitting the dirt, pushing off with my claws and moving so fast at times that even the trees around me seem to almost blur. There's such a peace in allowing my wolf to consume my actions for a while. It's like sitting in the passenger seat. You can hear and see everything, but you're not the one driving the car.

I also love watching our wolves interact. Roman and I are still in there, but they prance around together in circles, panting with their tails wagging. Even in my wolf form, he still towers over me, but you wouldn't know it by the way his wolf lets mine tackle him, pinning him to the forest floor. I can feel her excitement pulsing through me and his love through our bond. It's an absolutely incredible experience that I wish I could accurately put into words.

I've even been able to spend time with Khaos and Andrei, really trying to learn who my brothers are.

My soul-brother is so much different than my first impression led me to believe. Like Roman, I think he does it on purpose. If he doesn't get attached to people, then they can't disappoint him later. He loves nineties rock and heavy metal music. He plays drums as a hobby as well as a form of exercise and release. He's not sure what all he wants to do after he retires from hockey, but he really seems to be at peace with his decision. The way he's talked about it, I don't think he ever really loved hockey the way some of them do. I think it was always just an outlet that also happened to let him beat the shit out of people, my mate included.

My twin, on the other hand, is every bit my other half as is my mate, in obviously very different ways. Andrei seems to be the yin to my yang, opposite in so many ways. He only likes hot coffee while I prefer iced. He doesn't care for television or movies but agrees to watch stuff with me when I ask. Where I need structure and things to make sense, he likes to fly by the seat of his pants. Sometimes I just catch him looking at me similarly to the way Roman does…like I might disappear if he blinks. I can't imagine what he went through his whole life. He was forced to live his life without his parents because he could be stolen from them too. He was raised knowing his twin sister was kidnapped, making it his life's mission to find me. It probably doesn't help that I haven't been ready to accept the letter from our parents. As much as I want to, I want to be able to enjoy the words that they wrote for me, and with everything we're constantly facing, that doesn't feel like it will happen any time soon. He swears they'll love me, but there are too many what-ifs pinballing through my brain.

Roman managed to surprise me again by arranging a girl's weekend for me. He even went as far as taking the men to the pack to spend time with them and introduce Khaos to Brutus and the others. Runa, Zoey, Matilda, and I had the townhouse to ourselves for nearly forty-eight hours. Fran was, of course, hovering around somewhere just in case. We had one whole day that we designated as our Spa Day and pampered ourselves with all kinds of 'girly shit,' as my mate calls it. The second day was spent gossiping while movies played in the background. We finally finished Runa's Twilight lessons, and I've never seen her laugh so hard. It's always my favorite watching people watch the last movie. I'll never forget the entire theater gasping when we got to the part that we all know oh-so-well that turned into a complete plot twist. Chef's kiss. Runa didn't see it coming, and it was all just so carefree and fun.

He definitely knew what he was doing. Allowing me time to unwind before I spend the next however long wound so tight; I don't know how I'll function, but I'll get through. We have to do this.

The dark witch still refuses to speak after all of the men's interrogation tactics that I do not want the details of. Willa also tried to help to no avail. I think she's being brought with us on our trip and brought in front of the witch council to see if they can help us find out what's going on and who they're working for...or with.

"Why must you always think so loudly?" Roman grumbles into my ear, effectively scaring the shit out of me.

I squeal and leap into the air. When I realize it's him, I laugh and swat at him. "How can someone so large sneak up on people without being heard?"

He throws his head back, freely laughing, and I'm taken aback by the beauty of him. Hearing him laugh and seeing him smile fills my tummy with butterflies, my body stops working, and I can't help but just stare at him.

When his attention returns to me, he notices the way my eyes are devouring him. "Come now." He smiles. "You must finish packing. You've put it off long enough," he finishes, kissing the top of my head and making his way into the bathroom.

And how exactly am I supposed to focus on packing when he is so good at distracting me?

He snorts from the bathroom, telling me that, once again, my thoughts made it to him through our bond.

When I've finally finished packing, filling all three pink hard case suitcases that Roman bought for me, I smile at the accomplishment, but my stomach churns with thoughts of our trip.

Chasing the worry away, I head back to the kitchen to be with everyone. We decided to have another family dinner since we'll be apart for so long. Just as I almost set myself onto the barstool to watch the way Miss Tilly flits around the kitchen, the doorbell chimes.

That should be Khaos. "I've got it!" I shout. Benny throws me an ornery smile, and we both bolt for the door for no reason other than to have fun. He's way faster than me, but I still beat him because he's a sweetheart and lets me win sometimes. I smile up at him as I reach for the door, letting Khaos in. "Hey, Squirt!"

I beam up at him. I didn't care much for the nickname at first, being sensitive over my size for no reason. Instead, I've decided to fully embrace it. "Hey, Draq!" I spout back, biting my lip to try not to laugh.

Benny and Khaos look at me like I have two heads as Roman joins us, still by the door.

"Draq?" they all three ask in unison, making me lose control of the laugh, and it spills past my lips.

"Well, you call me squirt because I'm little. So, I decided I'll call you Draq because you've got those dark vibes, and you're old as fuck."

The space erupts into laughter, even Khaos'. He pulls me into his body once more, giving me a soft noogie and messing up my hair, but I can't be bothered to care.

Khaos keeps me tucked under his arm as we head back towards the kitchen, Roman taking his place on my other side.

Our big family dinner went much more smoothly this time.

Even Eris didn't look totally miserable tonight. We talked and ate the most delicious spread of American-style Italian food. The stuffed manicotti was my favorite pasta, and I could easily eat my weight in those breadsticks. Olive Garden's got nothing on Miss Tilly.

With our bellies full, the chatter around the table slows, and my heart hurts that we all won't be together. For them, it'll only be a week. For us, it'll feel like three.

"I'm gonna miss you guys." My voice cracks as I look around the room at our family.

Miss Tilly's eyes water with mine, and Runa smiles sadly.

Roman pulls me from my chair and onto his lap, wrapping his strong arms around me and making me feel so safe and loved.

"We'll miss you too, but you're going to have way more fun than you think," Runa speaks up. "I've heard Sabbax is stunning. You might be on a mission for information, but don't forget to have a good time," she finishes with a large encouraging smile.

"She is right about their realm being a sight to behold. You did pack all your camera gear, didn't you?" Andrei asks.

"I did." I nod. "Roman made sure to add it to my packing list for me…Runa, would you mind texting and checking on Zoey while we're gone? I told her we wouldn't have reception where we are going, but I don't want her to be totally alone if she needs anything."

"Of course. We already exchanged numbers."

Nodding and thinking to myself to make sure I'm not forgetting anything, I try to remain calm and not show what I'm doing. Speaking through the pack link, focusing on only Roman and Dolos, *Dolos, please really work with your brother while we're gone. Runa's heart hurts, and she's not going to sit around and wait forever.*

He flinches slightly at my words, and Roman pats my thigh in approval when Dolos' words reach me, *I have been, and I will find a way to get through to him. I feel like I've been making progress. Trust me, Runa isn't the only one hurting through this.*

I break character, no longer caring about being inconspicuous, to smile softly at him and offer him a small nod.

"All right, enough of that," Roman announces as he sets me on my feet to stand. Before I can even think, I'm picked up and heaved over his shoulder. "We should all get some rest. We have an early morning tomorrow," he says calmly, like I'm not kicking and squealing at him to put me down. I can feel his humor skipping down our bond as he turns to leave the room.

32
ROMAN

Our alarm goes off before the sun has risen. Leera pops right out of bed, clearly wound too tight. She slept fitfully, twitching in my embrace with her eyes darting around beneath her lids, and waking multiple times, worried we'd miss our alarms going off.

Groaning and stretching my body, I rise from the bed, much slower than my little mate did. When I've finished scrubbing my hands all over my face, trying to rub the tired away, Leera is nearly drooling as she takes me in. It took a few orgasms to get her to sleep last night, but she's still always starved for me. My morning wood bobs as I walk towards her, tapping her on the nose to break her from the spell of her dirty thoughts. "You're the one that said, and I quote, 'We won't have time for your shenanigans in the morning,' Princess." I dramatically cock my hip and point at her like she does to me.

She breaks into a small fit of giggles, so I scoop her into my arms and carry her to the bathroom for us to get ready for the day ahead of us.

Leera, Benny, Andrei, and I will meet Willa, Fran, and the dark witch at the private plane to take us to Triora, Italy, where the riftgate to Sabbax is located. Willa will have the witch spelled into unconsciousness until we reach Sabbax where we will hand her off to the royal guards and explain that we'd like to bring her before the council.

When we've both dressed in comfortable clothes for the long flight and packed our personal bags full of things we might need that we didn't want to pack in our suitcases, Leera scans her eyes across our room. I don't know if she's running through her mental lists and hoping she hasn't forgotten anything or if she's taking in the space because she'll miss it. "Ready, Princess?" I ask gently.

"I…you know…I think I am." She finally smiles that radiant and happy-without-worry smile. "Let's go have an adventure."

To be continued...

Acknowledgements

Would you look at that? Little Miss I-Could-Never-Write-A-Book just finished her third, and it's not slowing down any time soon. I have so many ideas pinballing in my brain for this series, another series on the back burner—though burning hotter and hotter for my attention—and a surprise for the end of the year.

We'll also be diving into audiobooks this year, and I can't wait!!

At the risk of sounding like a broken record, I'm so freaking thankful for every single one of you, every single page read, every single review written, every single rating posted, and every single recommendation.

I never had any idea how much love and support my little story and I would receive from the most amazing community.

Time for the Thank-Yous!!!

Daniel & Di—It's always the two of you first. My best friends. My rocks. My soulmate & my soul sister. Y'all push me to be better and support me with every crazy new idea I get. I'd be lost without each of you.

Lilly, my teenage daughter—Thank you for keeping me accountable and never letting me feel too cool.

My Omegas, my street team—I don't have adequate words to really tell you all what you mean to me. Some of you have been with me since My Pucking Mate was still a rough draft and didn't even have a name. Some of you joined as recently as yesterday. Each and every single one of you mean so much to me. The support you've shown me and the world I've created is more than I could have ever imagined.

Jaquelyn & Aurelia, my editor & formatter—The two of you are absolutely irreplaceable. You help me prepare the words I've cultivated for the world and wrap it in the prettiest packages for everyone to enjoy.

Thank you to M.E. Kelley @TwistedAndTriggered—I don't know why writing a blurb is so hard for me, so I'm so thankful you took my wimpy little blurb and turned it into its own little masterpiece.

A special thank you to some of my new author and author-related friends I've made since I published my last book—Sarah Jaeger, LO Gold, JP Sina, Moonlight Muse, Stephanie Light, Chardonae Davis, and so many more!

One more feral acknowledgement real quick before I let y'all go. To my amazing team members that helped me pay for the commission of two art pieces of Roman & Leera: Eva @angelicwicked, Marissa Renteria, Karlee Daniels, @herladyships_library, Chantel, Leslie King, Erin Cooper, Danielle Pettyjohn, @kristynlovesbooks, Althea Ball, Colleen Pupke, Sarah Whitley, Desiree Johnson, Megan Bailey, Ashley Hodges, and Candace Parnell.

About the Author

Hey y'all, Izzy here!

Still a Midwest mom of four.
Still working full-time in the real world.
Still reading, writing, traveling, walking, & shopping.
Still on Instagram & TikTok under IzzyElliottWrites.
Izzyelliott.com for PR Boxes, Signed Books, Pucking Were-
wolves Merch, and so much more!